TERI WOODS

Tell Me Your Name

Eric Enck

TERI WOODS PRESENTS

Tell Me Your Name

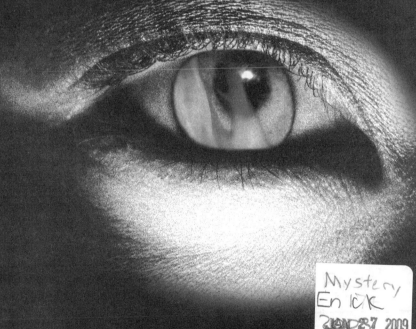

Eric Enck

This novel is a work of fiction. Any resemblances to real people, living or dead, actual events, establishments, organizations and/or locales are intended to give the fiction a sense of reality and authenticity. Other names, characters, places, and incidents are either products of the author's imagination or are used fictitiously, as are those fictionalized events & incidents that involve real person and did not occur or are set in the future.

Published by Teri Woods Publishing
Greeley Square Station
P.O. Box 20069
New York, NY 10001-0005
www.teriwoods.com
www.teriwoodspublishing.com

Library of Congress Catalog Card No: 2004097094
ISBN: 0-9672249-5-0
Copyright: November 28, 2003
File No.: TXU 1-147-544

Tell Me Your Name Credits:
Written by Eric Enck
Edited by Barbara Colasuonno
Manufactured by Malloy Lithographing
Text formation by Group 33
Cover concept by Dawn Hardy
Cover design created by Group 33 and Lucas Riggins
Cover graphics by Group 33

ACKNOWLEDGEMENTS

I would like to thank the lord above for helping me through the trials and tribulations of life.

I would also like to give respect to the following people:

Shirley Beck, my mother, who is a saint among angels and clearly the E in english; Johnna, my wife, who I was ever so blessed to meet and who stuck by me as I knew she would. We have a beautiful son together, and I thank her for him. Mason, as you grow, I hope you live to understand the society you dwell in and see that your father isn't nearly as insane as some believe. I love you, son. Johnna, I appreciate you giving me the will to never give up and to never look back down a broken road. You are my beloved and the beginning of all things wonderful; my agent, Chuck, who, with his determined perseverance of demanding the best, made it possible for me to unleash the flame; my father-in-law, John, who kept pushing...pushing; Phyllis Stalling, the other editorial genius, who helped me more than she will ever know; the guys at work who kept me in line and laughing through the painstaking hope — Richard, Bill, Harold, Robert, and Don the Knod.

All my nightmares that filter in the window at midnight. Such wonderful stories come from them.

Latoya, whom I was so pleased to meet in New York, and her wonderful insight; Barbara, the Editor of editors. If the world only knew how excellent you are, it would never be the same. It is an honor to see your magic come to life. And I hope to see it again; Dawn who, like your name, begins the day, every day. I look forward to your voice every time and think of the next time I will hear it again. All the work you've done in the production will never go unnoticed. I am in your debt; Teri Woods whom I can't say enough wonderful things about. You have my highest honor of respect. Your life mirrors your wisdom, Teri, and all the great endeavors you open for writers like myself. I have learned a lot from you and am honored to be part of such a powerful publishing company; my brother Robert Longenecker (you know who you are, bro). I hope our years ahead are good ones, and I hope no one ever gets on the bad side of your road because you are a very different kind of car, brother. A very different kind, indeed; and last but not least, my other brother, David Longenecker. Without him none of this would have come to be.

Thanks to all who have decided to read this novel and give me a chance to show what true terror is all about.

Scared...is a new word, my friend.

Eric Enck

Prologue

Unfamiliar scents mingle with the one he has been yearning to smell again. He can barely keep a thought in his head as he waits.

He likes to watch.

He breathes heavily in this strange place and bites down firmly on his lip to suppress a growing anxiety that will surely give him away. Blood begins to flow. He licks his lips and tastes its sweetness. He rocks back and forth on hard-soled shoes like a child anxious to ride the merry-go-round.

She enters the room on long caramel-colored legs. A pink towel covers her hair but the rest of her is perfectly visible. He silently retreats further into the closet so she will not see him. But his excitement is too great, and he steals another glimpse of her. He does not want to get too excited. He does not want it to happen again like the last time.

And the time before that.

But it is too late. He has grown hot and hard inside his pants.

Whispering words no living being on earth has ever

heard, he closes his eyes and remembers the woman he is in search of. So many years have passed, but he has not given up.

As she towel dries her hair, she hears a voice both distant and near. An icy finger of fear touches her at the base of her neck. She snaps her head up and instinctively covers herself with the towel.

"Tell me your name," the voice demands, very clearly, from over her left shoulder.

She turns to see the owner of the voice and stares into the face of a nightmare.

"Tell me your name," he again insists, and she does.

"Cassandra."

It is not the name he wants to hear.

As she looks up at his face, she is acutely aware of her beating heart. His eyes swallow her, and she becomes entangled in their blackness like she is captured in a net.

The man grabs her throat in his powerful hands, lifts her up and bites into her flesh. In one swift motion, her neck is torn open. He howls in animalistic lust and in abject disappointment as he ejaculates.

His release does nothing to quench his thirst.

As her blood coats the walls and sprays onto his face, he rips off his pants and pulls her dead body onto his.

He rapes her until the sun rises and it is again time to continue his search.

Like the last time.

Chapter One

A group of DEA agents sit in a white van across the street from Willie Zigs' apartment. It is three down from Cassandra Evans', a woman who lies dead in the dark of her living room.

The agents are communicating inside the van while tactical specialist, Tad Stevens, dresses in a tan suit. A microphone is placed in his ear by Sergeant Fielding.

"Now Tad, when you see Willie, remember to say nice to meet you. Got that? We're blind in here. We can't see you. And don't forget, your name is Jack Vender, with Hazzle Vacuum Cleaner Company."

"Yeah, I got all that," Tad Stevens (A.K.A. Jack Vender) replies. He grabs the shiny chrome vacuum cleaner and opens the side door of the van.

Inside apartment three-zero-four is a black man with dread locks. His right eye is filmed with gray blindness, and his left is crazed in highness. He has just snorted two lines of cocaine with a small, half-naked Mexican girl who is tripping on crystal methamphetamine. In the smoky apartment, in front of the television set, stands another black man who weighs three hundred pounds and has an ugly scar running deep down under his left eye. His name is Goody.

"How's the shit?" Goody asks Willie who is now smoking a cigarette.

"Pretty mutha fuckin' good, man," Willie replies.

"Whad de fuck, man?" Willie asks. "What's the weight on this shit anyhow?"

"Like I fuckin' know, man. I'm just the delivery boy."

Cortos, who is really Michael Simmons from uptown Shallow Front, walks into the living room. He is an eighteen-year-old drug dealer. Across his shirt is the remnant of a naked woman sucking on a lollipop. He wears an afro with a comb stuck in the midst of it. Beside him linger three other thugs. Six people in all, all smoking dope.

"Would you mind, bro?" Goody asks Willie who is looking down at the young Mexican girl.

"Go ahead," Willie answers, and Goody shakes the girl awake. In the next moment, he is walking with her down the hall to the back bedroom.

"Be out soon, after I make this bitch scream," Goody chuckles.

Willie laughs as rap music blares out of the sound system.

Suddenly, the doorbell shrilly rings.

Willie Zigs wildly turns his head. "Cortos! Get the fucking door!" he orders.

Two apartments down from Willie Zigs, a door opens. Hillary Frymer steps into the morning sun. Her hair is in curlers, and a robe sheaths her body. She is barely able to walk since her hip surgery. She fears that in another year or two, she won't be able to take small steps much less large ones. Looking towards the sun, she grimaces. Wrinkles age her forehead.

Being seventy isn't much fun. Bending for the newspaper, she hears her ancient knees pop. Midway down, she stops as she notices that Cassandra Evans' apartment door is wide open.

Hillary looks around cautiously. She bends a little to the left, trying to see inside the apartment. Of course, she has no idea that a drug bust is about to transpire two doors down. She also does not know what she will find when she walks across the way to Cassandra's apartment.

"Who the fuck are you?" Cortos asks as he stares at a tall man with brown hair parted to the side holding a vacuum cleaner.

Tad extends his hand. "Good morning. My name is Jack Vender with Hazzle Vacuum Company. I was wondering if you would be interested in seeing how our new products work, at no cost and no obligation," he says exactly as rehearsed in the van.

"Vacuum *cleaner*, isn't that what you mean?" Cortos asks.

In the cramped van, Fielding listens to the mic in his undercover agent's ear and thinks, *Just say it, Tad. Willie has got to be in there.*

"Look white boy, we don't need no mutha fuckin' vac..."

"WHO THE FUCK IS THAT AT THE DOOR?!" A voice yells. Cortos is cut off from what he is trying to say.

"It's nothing man. Just some vacuum cleaner fucker."

In the living room, Vender sees the man they have been looking for. A man wanted for kiddie rape, attempted murder of a federal agent and supplying most of Garrison its drugs.

Willie Zigs stops at the front door. He shows Vender his face and that insidious eye.

"Who the fuck you work fo?" Zigs asks.

"The policcceeeeeee," a voice whispers in Zigs' ear. Willie turns around to see where the voice is coming from. *Maybe it was the wind.*

"Hazzle Company," Vender responds.

It is the first part of the cue the police in the van are waiting to hear. Willie is in sight. They will hear the rest. *Nice to meet you.*

"Nice to meet you," Vender says, holding out his hand, his ear mic picking up and sending the words back to the van.

Willie stares at Vender for what seems like forever. He wants to ask Cortos who is standing beside him, if he hears the same voice that keeps invading his thoughts.

The van door crashes open. Eight tactical police officers and three DEA agents run in covered formation to the house. The agents veer to the left and run around to the back of the house. None of them notice a man wearing a black pinstripe suit and a broad brimmed hat on the other side of the street.

He likes to watch.

Willie does not respond to Tad Stevens. Instead, he pulls at his low-hanging jeans and flashes the gleaming chrome pistol grip of a nine millimeter. Tad sees it and dives off the porch into the bushes.

Willie pulls out the handgun, his head filled with the terrible voice. *Kill them all black man, for I am the one who holds the leash to all the wolves waiting for them.*

"FUCKING PIGS!!!" Willie screams as he fires the gun into the bushes.

Bullets slam into the front porch. Cortos runs inside. The bullets are coming from the cops.

As Cortos runs through the apartment to the back door, two tactical police officers run up the steps carrying a battering ram, the word HELLO painted on its front. They slam the ram into the door, and the hinges explode off the frame. Cortos stops dead in his tracks and turns as cops fill the kitchen. He runs down the narrow hallway to the bedroom where Goody is banging the Mexican girl. The look of terror on Cortos' face stops Goody mid-bang. He rolls off the naked girl, drops to the floor and reaches under the bed for his nine millimeter.

Beside the bed, Goody waits for the cops, and Cortos dives into a corner. Cortos grabs a box from under the bed that contains a thirty-eight pistol. But before he can open the lid, he is shot twice in the arm and thrown to the floor.

"STAY WHERE YOU ARE NOW, MOTHERFUCKER!!" Agent Ramirez yells. He is aiming a riot shotgun at

Goody whose hand rests on the trigger of his pistol under the bed.

"HANDS!! LET ME SEE 'EM, NOW!"

"Fuck you," Goody smirks as he tries to lean far enough back to take aim at the cop. His error is fatal. Ramirez fires, and the shotgun blows Goody's right hand into fragments of bone and bloody flesh.

Goody falls back, screaming.

"No habla ingles," says the Mexican girl, who is immediately handcuffed.

Tactical agents flooded the apartment. Two of the thugs managed to open fire on Fielding, who hurdled the living room couch. Bullets flew into the sofa so hard that puffs of cotton filled the air. They slowly parachuted back down to the floor. One DEA agent with an automatic machine gun, an MP-5, emptied an entire clip of bullets into the kitchen.

Plaster and drywall tore apart in the air. Six bullets slammed into one thug's chest, making him shake wildly in a death dance before he dropped to the floor. As another thug lifted his right hand to reload his pistol, a tactical cop shot him in the shoulder. A knob of bone suddenly appeared as the thug shrieked in pain.

The last drug dealer tried to run out the living room door. He opened fire on one of the SWAT agents, but a tactical officer behind the bathroom door surprised him and fired a shotgun at him. The thug's face disappeared. Bloody pulp splashed against the closet door as the thug fell sideways and dropped with a hard thump.

Zigs was still alive, pinned down and trapped in the kitchen.

Old Hillary heard the gunshots ring out but did not care. She stood in the doorway of Cassandra Evans' apartment and stared at the dead aquarium fish on the floor and the bloody glass shards. With her hands covering her open mouth, she tried to scream but no sound came out.

As her eyes followed the lines in the hardwood floor, she saw blood, too much blood. Then her gaze rested on its source.

A dead woman on the floor.

Hillary peered at Cassandra Evans. Her body was bent in a hellish position. She was laying on her back with her head propped against the lower part of the hallway wall.

Hillary couldn't breath. The shock of seeing a dead woman paralyzed her. So she just stood there, frozen in fear, as gunshots rang in her ears.

Suddenly, the woman began to move. Hillary's eyes grew wide as she watched Cassandra's head slid sideways down the wall. It hit the hardwood floor with a meaty thump.

It was then that Hillary finally screamed.

"COME ON OUT WILLIE! YOU'RE UNDER ARREST!" Agent Fielding yelled from behind the sofa. All the agents had drawn their guns, and all guns were aimed into the smoky kitchen.

"FUCK YOU PIG! YOU'RE A BLACK MAN! YOU SHOULD BE WITH ME, RUNNING FREE, MOTHER-FUCKER!!" Willie Zigs shouted as he lifted his face up to countertop level. After two minutes of silence and no response, a tactical cop out the window aimed his automatic weapon at Zigs' head.

"Watch out, Willie," the voice whispered.

Willie turn around once more and saw the cop aiming at his head. Before he could react, however, three bullets slammed into his jaw. One found his brain.

Agent Simon Fielding stood over Willie Zigs' dead body. Blood flowed from the gaping holes in his face, turning the white floors crimson.

"Job well done," Fielding congratulated his agents as they withdrew. From a search of the apartment, they uncovered large quantities of cocaine and other narcotics. Fielding was satisfied that he and his team had made a significant contribution to ridding Garrison and Shallow Front of their drug problems.

Two special agents escorted Cortos and the Mexican girl, the two survivors of the raid, into the morning sunshine. Fielding signaled for the local police to take over and another agent called in the coroner.

"Michael Simmons, you are under arrest for the use and distribution of illegal narcotics, for the possession of firearms and resisting arrest," Fielding said to Cortos as he escorted the criminal to a waiting police cruiser.

"You have the right to remain silent. Anything you say can and will be used against you in the..." Fielding stopped mid-sentence as he read Cortos his rights because in the background, he heard screaming. He scanned the area and spotted an old woman, panicked and out of control, running in the street.

"HEL... HEL...HELP!"

Fielding watched as curlers flew from her hair and landed in the street. Within ten feet of the police, she collapsed.

The police ran to where she fell. She was out of breath and shaking badly.

"Ma'am, what's wrong?" Fielding asked.

"Th...there's a wo...woman."

"Woman?" Officer Ramirez repeated.

"Dea...dead. I..I came running when I saw police cars."

"Who's dead?" Fielding asked.

"Dead...dead...woman!" Hillary cried, her eyes wild with nightmarish terror.

"Okay ma'am, just calm down. Where is she?"

"There. The door that's open, down the street," Hillary pointed with a shaky hand.

"Ramirez, call an ambulance for her. Officer Stevens, go over there and check it out. Take two officers with you."

"Yes, sir." Stevens replied. He motioned to the two nearest officers, and together they approached the apartment in question.

"Holy Christ," Stevens said as he crossed the threshold into Cassandra Evans' apartment. "We better call homicide."

The unnoticed man across the street disappeared into a strip of nearby woods. Leaves fell off the trees as he passed. Some died a natural end-of-summer death. Others from the close proximity to the man. Something within him made the wind whirl, the leaves fall to their deaths and the green grass turn brown.

I hold the leash.

Chapter 2

Detective Trent Holloway, a fifteen-year veteran of the Spring Garden Police Force, caught his reflection in a shallow puddle, a remnant from the rainstorm the night before. Bright green eyes, set deep into his strong brow, had lost their sparkle. Dark shadows under his eyes and good teeth stained yellow at the gums told him he was smoking too much. At thirty-eight, he was graying at the temples ahead of schedule, but his short, mostly black hair remained thick and wavy. In his reflection, he saw what the stress of his job had done to him. He didn't like it much.

When he looked up, he felt as if the world was watching.

He squinted in the bright morning sun. Droplets of rain that had not yet evaporated glistened on vibrant leaves. Summer was waning, and the foliage was just starting to change. Holloway understood how the leaves must feel, betrayed by the cruel joke nature plays on them. Rain and sun, then cold and death. Yep, Holloway knew exactly how they felt.

The dreams.

Every night for the last couple of weeks, Holloway had been having nightmares that twisted into the early morning hours and ravaged his sleep. The usual promise of a good night's sleep had been broken, and Trent didn't believe he could ever trust it again.

Behind him, the forensics team pulled up in their cold white van.

Detective Holloway breathed deeply, tossed his cigarette to the ground and followed them to the apartment. A sudden clap of thunder broke the eerie morning silence of the sky behind him.

As the team went to work, he remained on the porch and peered through the screen door. As seasoned as he was, as hard as his heart had become over the years, the scene before him was simply atrocious. The forensic photographer captured every angle of the horror with his blue flashing digital camera for all to relive over and over again forever. The rest of the crew carefully processed the scene, tagging and bagging everything and anything that might assist a prosecutor in sending the animal who committed the crime to prison, or better yet, to the death chamber.

After the initial processing was complete, Holloway opened the door and walked into the crime scene. Several strong odors overwhelmed him all at once, the strongest of which was blood. He noticed Officer Brian Gainesburgh choking back vomit, looking green.

"Officer," Detective Holloway said. The young officer looked up at the older man and tried to stand straight. "Maybe you should go outside."

"Yes, sir," a grateful Gainesburgh replied.

Yellow tape stretched from wall to wall across the hallway. Holloway stared at the words printed on it in black, CRIME SCENE, as he had done many times before. The blood on the floor in front of him had coagulated into a thick puddle. "Detective?" a female voice interrupted. Holloway turned. A young, eager forensics trainee waited behind him. He read the ID card clipped to her starched white shirt.

"Yes, Betty, what have you got?"

"Well, it appears to have been a crime of passion, sir. We believe the victim was raped. We also believe that she was strangled with this."

Detective Holloway peered at the plastic evidence bag held between the trainee's gloved fingers. A pink towel caked with dried blood screamed out 'weapon' from within its plastic confinement.

"And there's something else, too," Betty continued as she led the detective to the center of the living room. Holloway noticed dried blood on what remained of the aquarium.

"Letter A, here, is blood, blood from the victim. It appears that her attacker made his first move here. The lacerations on her neck indicate that she was stabbed, but by what, we don't exactly know. Letter B, these stains here, are being examined at the lab. We think, well we believe, that they are either vaginal secretion or semen."

"Time of death?"

"The coroner said somewhere between nine and eleven p.m. last night. But the autopsy will tell more. The medical examiner will be able to narrow that down, sir."

"Disturbing," Holloway muttered as he looked around the room. Glancing at the far wall, he noticed an array of books. His eyes grew large. Carefully, he stepped over the crime scene tape and went to the book shelf. "Betty, I want you to call the ME and ask him if the victim was pregnant. Let me know immediately," Holloway said.

"Yes, sir. But why would you think she was pregnant?" Betty asked as she watched the detective select a book off the shelf.

"Take a look at these books. Baby names, proper care of infants and toddlers, loving your child..." Holloway flipped through several of the books and read their copyright dates.

"These books are all new and purchased very recently. I believe that the victim may have been pregnant. And if she was, it could very well lead me in the direction of the father."

Betty looked at him oddly and was about to speak, but Detective Holloway spoke instead.

"Maybe he wanted to kill her because she was pregnant..." he thought aloud.

"Her husband's already got an alibi," a different voice drawled.

Holloway turned around to find Detective Frank Lion standing in the darkest corner of the living room. Flashes of fresh lightning reflected off his badge.

"Frank Lion," Holloway said and held out his hand to the sergeant from his precinct.

Detective Lion shook it.

"What did you say about his alibi?" Holloway asked.

"Last night, her husband, Brian Evans, was with his mother in Barrens. It's a little town just outside of Philadelphia. We've already established that he was there all week. Mr. Evans said he was working at the iron plant last night. We're checking his time card to verify. He apparently finished his shift at midnight. According to the coroner, the victim was murdered a few hours prior."

Detective Lion continued, "Philadelphia is almost four hours away by car. After speaking with the lad, he seemed genuinely upset by the whole thing. His reactions were normal."

Holloway turned back to the books. "I take it they were getting a divorce?"

"Yeah. Mr. Evans mentioned that. And he said something else, too. He believes she was seeing another man shortly before they split up, a Tommy, uh...uh.."

Holloway watched the twenty year veteran of the police force flip through his small notepad, searching for the last name. At the same moment, the front door of the victim's apartment swung open. A tall man wearing a tan trench coat walked toward both detectives.

"Colton. Tommy Colton."

Holloway turned to see Detective Jeremy Harris pushing past the door.

"And how do you know that, Detective Harris?" Holloway asked.

Lightning arced from outside, brightening the detective's face.

"We already have him in custody, Holloway. But don't get your hopes up. He's got a good alibi, too."

"Well then, we got a lot of work to do, don't we?" Lion said.

It was time to leave the rest of the investigation to the medical examiner. The autopsy was already underway and the scene had been processed. Holloway stood beside Detective Lion and jotted down thoughts in his own notepad. Lion was rubbing his flattop as he always did when he was thinking hard. Detective Jeremy Harris stroked his goatee. He liked to stay out late on his days off and was always the last detective on the scene when he resumed his schedule. He didn't ponder the cases as Holloway always did. Detective Harris was a seven to three man, and that was it. Any additional time spent on a case was considered charity, and he was not a charitable man.

A patrol car pulled onto the sidewalk near the apartment building. A patrolwoman looking for Detective Holloway got out and joined the activity at the apartment. Apparently the Detective's cell phone was not working.

"You know what Holloway?" Lion asked.

"What's that?"

"The guy who did this is fucking out there, like Jupiter."

"This really is some disturbing shit, Frank," Detective Harris said. All three men stood staring into the open bedroom closet.

He likes to watch.

"The perp hid in the victim's closet," Holloway announced.

"How you figure that?" Harris asked.

Detective Harris walked over to the closet and saw the black powder marks on the door near the knob, on the *inside* of the closet.

"I see what you're saying, Trent. Hey, do you smell that?"

"Smell what?" Frank Lion asked.

"I don't know, it...it smells familiar," Harris replied.

"I know. Like matches," Holloway said.

"Matches?"

"Yeah, Frank. You know the smell, like when you strike a match, then blow it out."

"That's pretty fucking..." Jeremy Harris started to say.

"Detective Holloway?" The patrolwoman had found him and waited outside the bedroom door.

Holloway simply looked over his shoulder. "Yes, officer?"

"The lab has been trying to reach you, sir."

"Excuse me, gentlemen," Holloway said as he left the room.

While dialing the medical examiner, Holloway thought about the pregnancy books and the blood on the floor. Whoever committed this horrible crime was on the loose. The clock was ticking.

It did smell like matches...

"Hello?"

"Yes, this is Detective Holloway with the Spring Garden Police returning your call. To whom am I speaking?"

"This is Chief Medical Examiner Derrick Moore, Detective. Thanks for getting back to me. Listen, you need to come down here immediately, sir. I'd rather not discuss why on the phone."

"Sure. I'm on my way."

Holloway walked out the door of the victim's apartment and into the humid late morning air.

Trent Holloway drove through a blasting rain. It fell in sheets of rage, it seemed. Oddly, the sky remained vibrant blue and the clouds bright white.

In the distance, purple lightning pierced the sky. The color reminded him of the diamond ring he adorned his wife's finger with last Christmas. Funny that such a memory should now pop into his thoughts as he drove on the long stretch of barren highway to the medical examiner's office.

It seemed to Holloway that he had taken this journey a thousand times before but always arrived at a different destination. No two crimes were ever the same and no two crimes ended up at the same place. Some never resolved themselves.

Few detectives have the satisfaction of bringing a criminal case to a conclusion. The road tends to be bumpy and pitted and just when you think it's smooth sailing, fog rolls in. ME Derrick Moore may have opened the window, but Holloway knew that he would have to roll it all the way down.

Every new case unnerved him. But this one was especially brutal. Holloway prayed that this new case, one of the most horrible abuses of humanity he had ever witnessed, be resolved, and quickly, because frightening him even more was the knowledge that a killer as deranged as this one rarely stops killing.

Chapter 3

The path leading to the front of the medical building was bathed in blinding white light. It bled out in long shadows between the foliage and reflected off the building's windows. The detective's heels clicked loudly on the hard marble floor as he approached the front desk. He flashed his badge at the clerk behind the window and signed in. The clerk smiled as she snatched the clipboard from him and signed her own name below his.

"Do you know where you're going, sir?" she asked.

"Yes, unfortunately I do."

"That's fine. Just remember to stay to the left at the bottom of the stairs. We wouldn't want you walking into the blood room now, would we?"

"Thank you, ma'am," replied Detective Holloway as he passed her, keeping to the right of the hall until it ended at a metal door. He opened it and went down the stairs.

Once on the lower level, Trent found Autopsy Room 2 and pressed the intercom button.

"Identification, please," a hollow voice requested.

"Spring Garden Police, Homicide Division, Detective Trent Holloway."

22

After a brief pause, the automatic lock disengaged. Holloway stepped into the room.

It was very large and very bright. A team of examiners worked intently at a central chrome table. A microphone wrapped in plastic hung from the ceiling. On the table lay the naked body of Cassandra Evans. One of the medical examiners approached the detective with his hand extended.

"Detective Holloway, a pleasure to meet you," greeted the compact, bald-headed ME. His name tag read DR. DERRICK MOORE. His smile was subtle, and his manner, though professional, was a little uneasy.

"What have you determined, doctor?" Holloway asked as he approached the corpse. Two members of the team looked up from their work and glanced at the detective.

Moore replied, "The subject is female, African American, age twenty-seven, eye color brown, hair black. No known diseases or complications prudent within diagnosis. We ran a blood test on her, all counts normal. There is no trace of poison or proximity."

"Notice the bluish contusions around her neck. These indicate..."

"Strangulation," Holloway interrupted.

"Yes, very good. She was strangled, but strangulation is not the cause of her death. This was done to her postmortem."

"Jesus." Holloway grimaced.

"Oh, it gets even stranger," Moore continued, "The victim was raped repeatedly after she was killed. She suffered lacerations and massive internal hemorrhaging from multiple stab wounds inside her vagina. We were lucky to find traces of seminal fluid. It is possible that her husband or lover was involved in her murder. I would like to get samples from both of them for comparison."

"We're not going to bother with tests at this time, Doctor. Both the men in her life have substantial alibis for the night she was killed."

"Yes, of course. Well then, Detective. Both of them are going to have to be notified that she was six weeks pregnant."

Feeling terrible as he did so, Holloway silently congratulated himself on his intuition. It was not right to see this woman laying on a slab of chrome, naked, shredded, with staples closing the wounds in her abdomen.

"Her attacker used a sharp instrument on her. He actually severed her intestines. I suspect the weapon was an axe," Dr. Moore said.

Detective Holloway could see her eyes from where he was standing ten feet away. They were dark and glossy and seemed to be peering at him from their emptiness, desperately seeking an answer. *Why? Why did I have to die, Trent? Why did you let me die?*

Dr. Moore continued with his findings. "The victim's throat was literally torn out."

"How do you mean?"

Detective Holloway watched from where he stood as the doctor approached the chrome table. Dr. Moore motioned to Holloway to come closer as he adjusted the victim's head to for better viewing.

"Her throat was chewed, not cut or lacerated by a blade, as we first suspected. This is difficult for me to say detective, but under the microscope, we found the imprint edges of teeth."

"Teeth?"

"Yes, sir."

"You're saying this fucker killed her with his mouth?"

"That's exactly what I'm saying."

"How big are they?"

"They are consistent with the size of lower incisors and canines of an Alaskan wolf." Moving to the victim's fingers, Dr. Moore said, "Ms. Evans managed to scratch her attacker before she was murdered. We found skin samples underneath her fingernails."

Holloway stared at the young woman's neck. Under the ligature marks from the strangulation, an open gash of flapping skin hung from ear to ear. Detective Holloway could see that the windpipe had been severed.

How would a wolf attack? By first tearing open the throat so its prey could no longer make any noises then continuing to maul the best parts.

"This was found in her mouth." Dr. Moore held an unfolded but heavily creased 5x7 piece of white paper between surgical tweezers.

Holloway hesitated. He looked down at the piece of paper, then at the writing. He slipped on a pair of latex gloves and gently took the slip of paper from the ME.

"You'll find it intriguing, I'm sure."

Detective Holloway walked over to a desk illuminated by a small flexible silver lamp. "Was this dusted for prints?"

"Oh yes, sir. We found a partial index finger print. It's being processed now."

Detective Holloway sat down at the desk, tugged the adjustable lamp closer and opened the note.

Dear police,

Even before I had looked into her eyes with great interest, I wish I could have captured this moment with a camera. But, alas, I do not own one. So I am at a loss.

It is in my own mind that I see us parading through hay fields of autumn color. Our love ever so short but still burning like our own views of melting sunsets to the handshake of shifting night. I see her before she sees me. This is important. This makes the difference. I see her before the darkness takes me that way again, surrounded by what she surrounds herself with. The darkness is different for me because I never stop seeing.

I sit here with my beloved beside me, as I am sure she is now beside you, on a silver examining table, yes? I sit here continuing to paint a picture of us. I draw fine lines of her in red flowers as I look into her empty eyes every so often. Most of what is left of her is now on the end of my brush and upon my easel. I dip my brush in her open throat again, the red calms me as I paint a picture of us together... down in hell.

Who will paint for me?

This was no wolf.

"Are you alright, Detective?" Dr. Moore asked as Trent hid the shivers that crept up his spine by distracting himself with a drawer containing plastic evidence bags.

"Call me on those skin samples as soon as you can, okay?"

"Absolutely, Detective Holloway," Dr. Moore said as the

policeman left Autopsy Room 2.

Holloway sat at his desk in Precinct 3, staring out the window as he had done so many times before. Detectives often lived in their own private hell, agonizing over the minute details of a crime, hoping to solve it.

"Tommy Colton was released a little while ago," Detective Frank Lion said as he threw a stack of paperwork on Holloway's desk.

"What's all this?"

"It's all we have on Cassandra Evans, the entire case file including your reports from the autopsy." Lion explained, "I don't know, Holloway. I think this is gonna be pretty cut and dry. You have a sexual predator here."

"What about the note, Frank? What about the note? I've never seen anything like it. It's downright creepy."

"It is pretty fucking gruesome. I gotta agree with you. Especially where it was found. Obviously, this guy is a complete psycho. And a werewolf. He's a twisted fuck, if you ask me."

"Is that all you have to say, Frank?" Holloway asked. "You think this is just your run-of-the-mill murderer?"

"He's probably some lowlife friend of the victim. Or maybe her ex-husband's friend. He obviously knew she was pregnant, that's why he raped her. He went a little too crazy. She wanted him to stop."

Detective Holloway turned away from Frank Lion.

Lion continued, "She struggled with him, and then he tore her throat out with his teeth."

"No, Frank. She was raped after she was mutilated."

"Even still..." Detective Lion lit a cigarette. "Pretty simple case if you ask me. The only thing that really bugs me is the sulphur smell in her bedroom closet."

Like burning matches.

"Dr. Moore thinks the assailant used an axe to butcher her."

"I still think it's standard."

"Garrison City has had its share of drug problems and homicides, but nothing like this. Frank, the ME's report shows that the teeth prints lifted off the victim's throat were made by something huge."

"So, some fucking creep is pretending to be a werewolf. We'll catch him, Trent. I'm not trying to be obtuse about it either."

"Coulda fooled me, Detective. Look, this woman was going to have a baby!" Holloway was frustrated by his colleague's attitude.

"I know, I know," Frank said and walked out of Holloway's office.

Detective Holloway remained in his office the rest of the afternoon, letting his mind mull over the facts of the case, facts that would undoubtedly shock the town.

Trent had not yet heard from the ME's office about the skin samples taken from under the victim's nails, and it would be at least another twelve hours before the FBI would have the fingerprint results. But in a few hours, fingerprints would be the least of Detective Holloway's problems.

28

Downtown, on the corner of a twisting old side street and a touristy new one, is a small pub. It is owned by a man with no morals named Gussby Lovern. Gussby grew up in this gloomy town serving booze. He likes undressing his female employees with his eyes.

Around the corner from Gussby's is a Chinese restaurant. It is the last stop before the road begins to wind its way up a steep hill.

The road, known as Mill Street, splits right and left a mile past WonTon's, and each side becomes its own one-way. The road was actually constructed around an acre wide and three acre long strip of land. In the middle of the strip is an overgrown stretch of grass where the remains of an old mansion sit. It used to be a hospital but a fire destroyed much of the structure many years ago. Trent Holloway had been a rookie.

East of Gussby's Tavern, Mill Street becomes lined with brick sidewalks and small suburban homes before emptying into the belly of the city. The tidy, quaint family homes are gone and are replaced with rundown apartment buildings, some with boarded-up windows, all with paint peeling from window and door frames.

Wilco Avenue intersects Mill Street in the heart of the business district. Further east, Mill ends at Calldown Boulevard. The well-to-do live at the far end of town in a small, private community. Detective Trent Holloway lives here.

The community center boasts an Olympic-size swimming pool with diving boards at one end and a shallow kiddie area at the other. The pool belongs to the residents of the private community. It is not at all like the public pool five miles away. On especially hot nights when the public pool is closed, city kids open up fire hydrants and run and splash through the cold spray. The private pool is available all the time.

Detective Holloway laid in bed next to his wife. Instead of holding her, he stared up at the ceiling. He was approaching forty, much wiser than his years, but still suffering from memories he wished were long dead.

Down the hall, his son, Detton, slept peacefully in his bedroom. Holloway envied the special innocence of his five-year-old son. He wished he was once again five with no worries in the world.

Trent rolled onto his side and wrapped an arm around his angel, his wife of seven years. He wondered how she managed to keep her wings hidden.

"I love you," she whispered.

"I love you too, Sheila."

Trent finally began to relax. He even felt groggy. But then he started to think about the killer. The terrible images from the crime scene intruded, and Trent could no longer keep his eyes closed. *A profiler from Capitol Hill would have a field day with this guy,* he thought. The detective began to imagine what the perpetrator looked like, a dark man with midnight black hair, tall and lanky...

That's your father, Trent, the man you are always thinking about. Why do you always give unknown killers your father's face?

Trent began to drift off to sleep, but the thoughts kept

coming. In those few moments before sleep overwhelmed him, two thoughts came to him: Cassandra Evans was pregnant. And the smell of burning matches.

What was that?

Trent dreamed that he was walking down the hall to Autopsy Room 2. But instead of white walls and floors, everything was bathed in red. Even the ceiling lights glowed red.

Trent walked for what seemed like miles, the heels of his hard dress shoes clicking like a clock on the floor.

His body tensed in his sleep as he approached the stairs. Slowly, he ventured down one step at a time.

Remember what the clerk said. Don't go into the blood room...

At the bottom of the stairs, he heard a sound. It was a low, raspy sound like a rattlesnake's vibrating tail. As Trent shifted in his bed, he walked towards the sound in his dream and saw a door bleeding white light from its seams. He noticed that he stood before door number 6, not number 2 of the autopsy room.

Holloway opened the door and shielded his eyes from the blinding light. Even though he was in a different numbered room, he was again standing in the same room he stood in earlier that day. Absent, however, was Dr. Moore and his crew. In their places were three Alaskan wolves prancing around a dead body splayed on the chrome table. Upon closer inspection, the detective realized that it was his own lifeless face staring back at him.

"No!" he screamed in his dream and took a few steps backwards.

One of the wolves heard him and snapped its head up. With frightening speed and agility, it leapt over the table and landed on paws as big as human hands not ten feet in front of him. Its yellow eyes looked directly into his, and it bared its long, stained fangs in a hideous grin. Impossibly, it spoke.

"Trent, my dear boy. What you see is what you'll get."

"Who are you?" Trent pleaded in a trembling voice.

"I am who you want me to be, Detective," the beast cryptically replied.

In another fantastic leap, it rejoined the pack. Then the three wolves fell upon Trent's dead body and began ripping it to bloody pieces.

Trent woke up then, shaking and sweating. Beside him, the sheets were rumpled but empty. Sheila had gone to work at the hospital.

As he scanned the bedroom, Trent's pupils were dilated and his eyes were glossy with the freshness of the nightmare. He stripped off his t-shirt, wiped the beads of sweat from his forehead and then tossed it across the room.

An unwelcome sliver of sunlight pierced his vision and announced that another day had begun.

Chapter 4

As the sun took hold over the morning, Detective Holloway's home phone rang. He let it ring twice as he poured himself a cup of coffee. The call was from an officer in the State Police Troop C.

"Detective Holloway, this is Sergeant Mike Grove from Garrison State Police Barracks."

"Good morning, Sergeant. What can I do for you?"

"Your supervisor, Captain Pullman, said it would be a good idea to contact you directly about this matter."

"And what matter would that be, Sergeant Grove?"

"Well, sir, we found a body out by Briar Creek. Are you familiar with the area?" Grove asked.

"Somewhat," Detective Holloway said as he lit a cigarette.

"The victim has been identified as Amanda Dawson, age thirty-two. From the looks of it, she's been dead several days. We've learned that she was in Garrison City three days ago, so we're guessing that she was killed there and then transported here. In a half hour, there will be a news report on television. I'm telling you all this to give you the heads up on the media attention, but I also believe that our cases may be related."

"How so?" Holloway asked.

"A note found in the victim's mouth, sir."

Trent was not happy that the sergeant knew the particulars of his case but didn't let on, preferring instead to just listen. "What did it say?"

" 'It begins.'"

" 'It begins?'"

"Yep."

"That's all?"

"Yes, sir. That's all the note said."

Trent thought about this piece of information for several seconds. "Well then, Sergeant. Let me ask you something. Was the victim pregnant?"

"Yes, sir. She was. It's odd you'd ask that, though."

"Our victim was pregnant, and I wanted to see how similar our cases really are," Holloway replied. "How was Ms. Dawson murdered?" he then asked.

"Well, sir, she was disemboweled, slit right down the middle. And some of her internal organs appear to be missing."

"Did I hear you right? Missing?"

"Uh, yes, sir."

"Jesus. Alright Sergeant. Thanks for the call. No doubt I'll be in touch soon," Holloway promised.

"No problem. There is one more thing I wanted to mention, Detective," Grove hesitantly said.

"Shoot."

"Well, we don't know if this is a big deal or not, but the forensics crew and I down here detected an unusual smell at the scene," Grove said.

"And what would that be, Sergeant?" Trent asked, already sure of the answer.

"When we walked the perimeter and established the crime scene, we didn't see anything to indicate..."

Holloway interrupted, "You smelled burning matches, isn't that right?"

"Well, yes, sir. That's exactly what we smelled. But it didn't make any sense," Grove replied.

Holloway froze. "How long did the smell last?"

"About two minutes. Do you know where the hell it might have come from?"

"Sergeant, I don't have a clue — yet. But it seems that that smell is a trademark of sorts of our perpetrator."

After a moment of silence, Holloway spoke again.

"Good day, Sergeant Grove. When you finish your paperwork, please fax my office what you've got on Ms. Dawson."

"I will, sir. You have a good day, too."

Detective Holloway hung up and drank the last of his coffee, which had gone cold, before walking into the living room. He turned on the television and watched the breaking news on Channel 6. He placed a blank tape into his VCR, pressed RECORD and taped the Amanda Dawson story, at least the parts that the police and press knew. The rest of it, Amanda took to her grave.

She stopped on the shoulder of the road to take a belly rub break, as she affectionately called it. Little Jason was kicking up a storm, aiming at her bladder, of course, and Amanda tried to shift him around a bit so she wouldn't pee in her pants. She had to go to the bathroom so badly and knew that she wouldn't make it back to Garrison City.

It was already late. The moon was high in the sky and in the little town of Lincoln, nothing was open. So she did what she usually did to relieve her discomfort and took a belly-rub break.

Amanda Dawson hadn't been stopped five minutes when a hand reached into the open driver's window.

Amanda's car was found in the brush ten hours later by a policeman on a routine patrol. The driver's side door was torn completely off its hinges and thrown into the woods. Blood and torn flesh led the police deeper into the tangled brush where they found Amanda face up, staring into the sun.

It begins.

"The communities of Spring Garden and Garrison City have been touched by evil," the Channel 6 reporter announced. "Indeed, these two peaceful small towns have been sadly reminded that they are no longer immune to the brutality found in the big cities."

As the reporter continued, the citizens of both towns learned two glaring facts about the cases — both woman were savagely murdered and both were pregnant.

Fear descended and those who may have taken life for granted before began to pray.

Before the nightmare that no one would ever forget

began, it could be said that Shallow Front and its hamlets, Garrison City and Spring Garden, were nice places to live. In summer, the town fairs and parades attracted tourists and helped the economy. In the fall, the Halloween Fair was a weekend-long event offering hayrides, pumpkin pies baking contests and a beauty pageant. And in winter, in addition to the customary Christmas festivities, the citizens made an effort to brighten the nights by participating in the Festival of Lights, a display in every window or door in the entire town.

There were no suspicious deaths last year in Garrison.

And there was only one in Spring Garden. A woman was found frozen to death in her car, buried in the snow, a victim of a car accident. Poor woman wasn't missed by anyone.

Lincoln is a tiny town that hangs onto the edges of the Hillside Mountains west of Shallow Front. No one lives there except Jacob Levey. He is an old man, blind in one eye from a hunting accident, not like Willie Zigs who's been blind since birth.

Three nights ago good ol' Jacob Levey went to bed early because of a sudden stomach virus. If he had stayed up and out of bed just a little longer, he would have seen a tall man dressed in dark clothing walk past his house just after midnight. The man wore a broad-rimmed, police-style hat that hid his face. Jacob would have seen him pass right outside the kitchen window.

And if anyone would have been looking at just the right

moment, they would have seen what Cassandra Evans and Amanda Dawson had seen. The face of evil making itself welcome and at home again in a town that had been all but forgotten its past. Evil had planted a seed long ago, and it was beginning to sprout.

At Gussby's Tavern, Darla Goodman stuck a piece of chewing gum in her mouth and tied on her waitress apron. In large red letters it read "You can stare all you want at Gussby's".

Parking a pencil behind her ear, she crumpled the gum wrapper and tossed it in the trash. She was ready to start taking drink orders.

The television over the bar was tuned to Channel 6. The reporter was back again, but with nothing new to report, he instead interviewed Cassandra Evans' family members. Cassandra's mother, with tears streaming down her face, talked about her daughter and her unborn grandchild, both dead at the hand's of a mad-man. Her brutal killer was still on the loose, and she feared for his next victim. All watching at Gussby's remained quiet in a respectful moment of silence until Billy Olsen asked Gussby to change the channel.

After that, more local folk entered the bar. They only had two things to talk about — Amanda Dawson and Cassandra Evans.

The truth was that something terrible had taken root in Shallow Front, something so terrible it can turn the sky black with crows leaving the comfort of their nests. Something growing like an insidious weed.

Shallow Front was rotting from the inside out like an apple does when a worm has made its way into the core. The exterior looks fine but the hidden center is ugly and evil.

In Shallow Front, the worm was a man, a man who waited and whispered, who remained unnoticed because he knew which dark corners to hide in, who knew how to be patient.

Long before Gussby's closed for the evening, a violent rainstorm swept over the city and caused a blackout. Detective Holloway read his case notes in his easy chair by candlelight. Every so often, exhausted by the case and the media and the incredible workload, his green eyes started to close. But Trent would jolt himself awake and plod on.

Detton was long asleep in his room, no doubt dreaming of colorful cartoons. Sheila was curled up under the blankets in their bed.

Soon it would be morning again. Soon the days would fall away to autumn. Soon darkness would come to Shallow Front much too early and stay much too long.

At Gussby's, Darla Goodman glanced down at her watch.

Break time!

"Hey, Gus!" Darla shouted.

"Whatcha want, hotcakes?" he shouted back.

"Do I got time for one?" she asked, giving the smoke

sign with her two fingers.

"You got ten minutes, dammit," he growled.

"Thanks, babe." *What an asshole,* she thought.

Darla opened the double doors behind the bar and teetered in her pink high heels toward the exit doors. Strands of her black hair had fallen loose from the bun at the nape of her neck.

Sifting through the pocket of her apron, she found a rumpled, half-empty pack of Newports and a book of Gussby's Tavern matches.

Shaniqua Holmes smiled as Darla tripped through the door with a cigarette stuck between her lips. Shaniqua was a middle-aged, black woman Darla just loved working with, especially on crazy nights like this. The combination of the heat and humidity brought out all kinds of weeds.

Standing beneath the roof's overhang, the two women gossiped and complained as usual.

"Fuckin' A! That fat bastard let you slam a nail? I can't believe it!" Shaniqua exclaimed.

"Sure did. He's being awfully nice tonight," Darla commented.

"That cracka ain't eva nice, girl. Only when he's gett'n his nuts blown off at the Vega," Shaniqua said with a sly smile.

"I didn't know Gussby liked peep shows." Darla's jaw dropped.

"Fuck, yeah, he does! And he does more'n peep, too."

Darla laughed. The Vega had almost been shut down recently. Rumors that the strippers were actually prostitutes got the police involved.

"Me and you should work over there, you know?" Shaniqua gave Darla the eyebrow. "What? That's a bad idea?" Darla asked.

"Maybe not for you! But sheeeit! Lookit me! With a body like this, I'd be lucky if I could get Gus to dig down deep enough to pull out a moldy dime!"

Both girls laughed and blew smoke through heir lips. These moments were their favorite parts of their shifts. Shaniqua had just gone through a long, difficult divorce. Her ex-husband had threatened and scared her. The news on the television had sent terror singing through her veins all over again. A murderer of pregnant women was on the loose. How could God let such a creature exist?

Darla's life was pretty uneventful compared to her friend's. She was a single mother with a little son, another example of poor, white, trailer trash. And although she said to herself many nights "I'm not really a slut", her reflection in the mirror said otherwise. She had taken money for performing certain services time and time again. *Just doing it to get by,* she told herself.

Sometimes, while she sat in front of the mirror, while little Michael slept, she wondered why she did it. And wondered why she would do it again. Even though she knew that she was selling herself short, she had convinced herself that she did it for the fifties and twenties men threw at her. Money she saved for Michael, to get him out of the trailer and into a real life.

But Darla was exhausted from telling herself that next time would be the last time. She worried that she hooked because she was addicted to it. And using Michael as an excuse was just another excuse.

If that damn Gussby would just give me a raise! But Gussby did her, too. And in spite of it all, it really wasn't all that bad.

"How are thangs with the little one?" Shaniqua asked as she flicked her cigarette and watched the storm darken the already dark sky.

"He's pretty good, been into those damn video games."

"Yeah, my nephew likes them fucking things, too," Shaniqua chuckled.

Suddenly lightning flashed like a million camera bulb going off at once, and the rain stepped it up about ten beats.

"We better get inside!" Darla yelled.

Both waitresses returned to the shelter of the tavern and went back to serving drinks. A brawl between Billy Warrington and Harry Loughton was simmering at the bar.

Across the street, a few steps out of the streetlamp's reach, a man waited and watched. His eyes were filled with madness and a hatred so deep that it had remained an inferno inside of him for more years than he could remember. He would not be satisfied until he found what he was looking for. And he would never give up the search. He had the patience of a saint.

He likes to watch.

"Alright guys, no fights in my bar!" Gussby yelled.

Harry, a long-haul truck driver with a huge gut from eating fast food on the road, and Bill Warrington, the troublemaker every town has, eyed each other from opposite ends of the bar.

"I ain't said shit to the little fella," Harry told Gussby. "Why's he looking at me like that?"

Billy pivoted on his stool and pointed his face in Darla's direction. "Hey, Darla! Tell Gus to make me one of them pink drinks."

"You mean a Purple Motherfucker?" Darla shot back.

"Yeah, one of them!" Billy laughed.

"OK, Bill." Gus said. "Why you wanna go and switch drinks now? You're doin' just fine with beer."

"Come on, Gus. Give me one a them 'fore I go on home," Billy whined.

"OK, Billy. One drink. You're up to no good. I can see it in your bloodshot eyes."

"Jesus Christ, Gus! All I want is a drink," Bill moaned.

"Maybe you should make him that pink drink he asked for in the first place. Pink is for pussies, after all," Harry said, smirking.

Bill jumped up from his seat and tried to edge pass Gus to Harry's side of the bar. Gussby didn't budge an inch.

"I'm telling both of you. Don't fuck up," Gussby warned.

"Say, Bill. What have you been doing with yourself lately?" Harry asked.

"Been fixing trailers. Skirting mostly. What's it to you?"

"What have you been doin'?" Harry repeated himself.

"Skirting, Harry, skirting. You deaf? Don't you know what a skirt is?" Billy asked condescendingly.

"Of course I do, Bill." Harry laughed. "I'm just surprised you ain't wearing one. It would go nice with that pink drink of yours."

Bill turned his blue menacing eyes on the truck driver, "When you grow a cock under that gut of yours, then you can speak to me that way."

"Hey, Billy. Fuck you. Don't..." Harry started.

Bill interrupted, "I'm not your buddy. And beyond that, you need not to speak to me at all."

Harry stood up and, like he was a beacon, all eyes were on him. Despite his beer belly, he looked particularly menacing. At six-feet-four, he sneered down at Bill and his purple drink.

"Why don't you get up, cowboy?" Harry threatened.

"GUYS! GUYS! I SAID NO FIGHTING! HARRY, SIT THE FUCK DOWN!" Gussby had one hand on each of the men, trying to keep as much distance between them as possible.

Harry chose not to sit. Instead, he reached past Gus and nudged Bill Warrington on the shoulder.

"Get up, you chicken shit piece o..."

But before Harry could finish his sentence, Bill sprang off his barstool, grabbed another patron's beer mug and brought it down hard on Harry's head. Shards of glass showered the bar and beer splashed all over Gus' pants.

"DARLA! CALL THE POL..." Gus shouted as he extricated himself from the tangle.

But Darla didn't run to the phone. She was frozen in place in fear as she watched Bill Warrington pull the largest buck knife she had ever seen from his side pocket. He lined up the tip of it to Harry's nose. Lights glinted off the razor sharp blade and sent sparkles around the room.

"I'm gonna carve my next meal, Harry. I'm gonna carve

it right off your gut. You'll finally be able to see your cock before I carve that off, too."

Harry had the good sense not to move a muscle.

"Do you understand me, son? Hmmmm? Who's pink now?"

"Bi-Bil-Bill, I'm sorry man. I didn't mean any of..." Harry tried to apologize.

"Well, I mean it, Harry. You got that, motherfucker?" Bill asked.

Don't waste your time talking, Bill.

"What?" Bill said to himself. He spun around the room, knife still in his hand, searching for the source of the voice.

"I didn't say anyth..." Harry protested.

"I WASN'T TALKING TO YOU, MOTHERFUCKER!!!" Bill screamed at Harry. Then, almost subconsciously, he dropped his hand to his side.

"I'm not gonna do it," Billy said as if in a trance, almost possessed. His eyes were hazy and lost, and he began mumbling unintelligibly.

"Who the hell is he talking to?" Darla asked Gussby.

"I don't know, Darla. I just don't know," Gus replied, equally perplexed.

Gussby watched as Bill backed up to the front exit. His body twitched and his head rolled around on his shoulders. He grabbed his head as if he was suffering a god-awful migraine and yelled at the ceiling.

"NO!" Bill screamed as he looked up. "NO! I won't do it, goddamn you!"

Do it now, Billy. You know you've wanted to for a very long time. Slice his throat, Billy!

The voice in Bill's head was gentle yet menacing and urgent. Bill swung around again to try and locate its source with the knife still in his hand.

"Billy, honey, why don't you put that knife down?" Darla gently urged but wished she hadn't. The sound of her voice brought Billy's lunatic eyes to focus on her. They looked like they would pop out of his skull. The rage inside was about ready to burst like a firecracker.

Tell her to shut up Billy. I don't like her voice.

"What's wrong wit you?" Shaniqua asked.

Billy didn't answer. And neither did the voice. Billy remained where he was, his gaze once again floating up to the ceiling.

Tell them all to shut up NOW!

"Billy, please. You're gonna hurt someone if you..."

"SHUT UP!" Billy screamed, startling everyone.

That's better Billy. Now, kill them all.

"No."

You better do what I say. Remember, I hold the leash.

"Noooo!!" Billy wailed.

Billy raised the knife to his face and held it in front of him. Darla thought he was lining up to charge Harry Loughton, but instead, Bill's eyes filled with sorrow and remorse.

"I'm sorry everyone," Billy said and a tear slid down his face.

"It's alright, Bill. Just lower the ..."

But Bill never gave Gussby the chance to finish his sentence. Dead silence engulfed the room like flames as everyone watched in horror as Bill Warrington flipped the knife around in his hand and sliced open his own throat.

"JESUS CHRIST BIIIILLLLL! NOOOOO!!!!" Gus howled.
"Oh my God! SOMEONE CALL AN AMBULANCE!"
Harry Loughton yelled.

Billy Warrington fell down beside his knife. Blood
pooled around his body, pouring from his throat like
water from a broken faucet. Some blood splashed onto
his lips. He looked like he had kissed the floor. The
incongruity of the bright colors of the neon lights reflect-
ing off the deadly steel of Bill's bloody knife made Darla
scream.

Officer Squall was the first to arrive at the scene.
Talking with Gussby Lovern and the two dozen other witnesses, he easily determined that Bill Warrington had
committed suicide.

The paramedics arrived too late of course. And then the
coroner came to release Billy Warrington's body to his
family. A half hour later, Detective Holloway walked
through the front entrance into Gussby's Tavern.

"So according to the waitresses and the owner, this guy
started talking to himself?" Holloway asked incredulous-
ly.

"Yes," Officer Squall replied.

"Then he cut his own throat?"

"Yes, sir. That's what happened," replied Officer Squall,
clearly uneasy.

"Well, then, thank you Officer. That will be all."

Detective Holloway passed the pool of blood that was
beginning to congeal on the floor. Gus had gone to get a
mop and bucket. And Frank Lion walked in.

"Detective Lion," Trent said as he saw his colleague.

"Hey, Holloway. How's it going?" Lion asked.

"Well, Lion, tell me, is it me or is there something awfully strange going on in this town?"

"I know. I don't get it either," Frank Lion replied, clearly puzzled by Bill Warrington's death.

"Let's think about it. Why would a man commit suicide like this?" Trent asked as he gestured to the blood on the floor.

"And in this place," Detective Lion added.

"Witnesses say he was fine. He was getting ready to fight Harry Loughton. Stab him actually. Then... then he went into a daze and never recovered. I don't get it," Holloway said, obviously troubled. "People just don't commit suicide in public."

Frank agreed. "I know. When they want to off themselves, they don't want anyone around to try and talk them out of it. But, you knew Billy. He had a couple of loose screws rattling around."

The detectives walked the bar, trying to figure out what they never would. After ten minutes, they released the remaining few witnesses. Holloway knew that they would add nothing new to the story.

Shaniqua and Darla walked to their cars together.

"Well, honey, I think I have had enough for one night. How about you?" Darla asked.

"Believe me," Shaniqua said, "I ain't neva comin' back here."

"Yeah, I think Gussby will close the place down for a

few days."

"I threw up twice," Shaniqua confessed.

"I know. I saw you. Jeez! Gus wanted me to call the ambulance, but I couldn't," Darla said. She stopped by her car and started to cry. "Jesus... Jesus, Shaniqua," Darla sobbed.

"Now, now, kiddo. There wasn't nuttin you could do anyway," Shaniqua told her friend.

"I'm sorry," Darla said, pulling herself together. "I just never saw anything like that before."

"Me neitha. And I neva want to again! But don't worry any more about it. It's gonna get better," Shaniqua promised as she hugged her friend.

"How?" Darla asked, wiping her face.

"Well, we sure don't have to worry 'bout them two fighting anymore, now do we?"

"No. I guess not." Darla saw the humor in what Shaniqua said but couldn't find it in herself to laugh. It was all just too sad.

Turning around, Shaniqua opened her car door while Darla stood with images of Billy Warrington's suicide swirling in her head.

"Anyway, I think I'm gonna look for another job, hon. Starting tomorrow. What do you think?"

There was no response.

"Darla?" Shaniqua turned around. "Darla?!"

Darla was standing by her car, not hearing what Shaniqua was saying. She looked across the street and her vision became hazy, like she was trying to see across a smokey room.

"Girl, you okay?" Shaniqua asked as she tugged on her

friend's elbow.

Darla snapped out of her trance. "Yeah, I'm fine. Thought I saw something, that's all. No biggie."

A tall figure had been standing very still across the road under the streetlight. The yellowish-green glow from above outlined his dark shape but didn't illuminate his face at all. His long shadow stretched across the road, and even though he was at least fifty yards away and she couldn't see his eyes, Darla was mesmerized by them. They gleamed a horrid red, like two bright embers in the midst of fire.

Then he was gone.

"I'll see ya tomorrow." Shaniqua said.

"Yes, se..see you tomorrow."

Shaniqua drove home, not liking the look in Darla's eyes.

Darla locked her car doors for the first time ever and drove home.

Holloway woke up the following morning with a fever. It didn't take a detective to figure out that Sheila had carried home from the hospital an unwanted germ. He grabbed the aspirins from the medicine cabinet and downed two with a glass of water. After his shower, he started to feel like himself again.

As he dressed, his mind turned to the Evans and Dawson cases. Something had been nagging at him, and he was finally able to put his finger on it. He came to believe that the perpetrator wanted the police to have his fingerprints. Detectives Lion and Harris would think he was crazy because it was only a hunch. But most serial killers would be too smart to leave fingerprints. And that was exactly what their perp did — on the inside of the closet door.

As Trent pulled his pants on, he felt dizzy again. *I guess the aspirin didn't do the trick,* he thought. Chills rushed through him and and he felt queasy.

"Oh boy, I'm really not feeling too well," he said aloud to himself and threw his pants on the bed. *I still have a few sick days left.*

Detective Holloway fell back on the bed.

He cut his own throat. Cassandra Evans' was torn out. Could these cases be somehow related? Was it Bill Warrington who murdered Cassandra Evans and Amanda Dawson? And then, in remorse, decided to kill himself?

Holloway called in sick.

That afternoon, as Detective Jeremy Harris drove down Calldown Boulevard and scanned the crowds of people walking along the sidewalks, he began to feel uneasy.

He actually ripped the girl's throat out?

The citizens of Shallow Front went about their daily routines as if nothing was wrong with the world. But Harris felt that something was changing, and he became acutely aware that life in his town would not return to normal any time soon. He decided then to assist Holloway on the murder cases and put to paper his own thoughts and theories.

I don't feel so well, Harris thought.

As he pulled up to the precinct, Detective Harris opened the door and vomited.

Holloway tossed and turned in bed. Vivid dreams assaulted his slumber.

He once again found himself walking down the same hallway in the medical building. He was again drawn to the white light bleeding from the autopsy room door. The door still read 6.

He expected to see the wolves prancing around his dead, decaying body. But this time he saw Cassandra Evans, motionless as the coffin she now permanently rests in.

Her naked body was prone on the steel gurney. The blue hue from the overhead lights tinted her skin a sickly gray. Then, very suddenly, as if the top of her head was being pulled by an invisible string, she sat up.

"Trent!" she screamed. The shrill sound of her voice deafened Holloway and filled his mind with terror.

Her eyes were completely black. The whites had been obliterated. Holloway could see his reflection in the glossy blackness. And upon closer inspection, he could also see the door behind him slowly closing. He was going to be trapped in this room with...

"Trent. Why did you let me die? Trent?" Cassandra asked. "Why did you let him kill Billyyyyyy?"

Her words sounded like a poor recording on a warped machine.

"Please," Trent begged as he closed his eyes in his dream. "I don't want to see anymore."

Upon opening them, Cassandra was in front of him, a lip's kiss away, with death on her breath.

"He holds the leash!" she shouted.

Maggots crawled on her tongue and danced in her open throat.

"Trent, wake up!"

Holloway was jolted awake, gasping in fright. But standing before him in the shadows of his bedroom was his wife.

"Honey... Captain Pullman is outside."

"What time is it?" he asked.

"Two-thirty in the morning."

"What does he want?" Trent asked.

"I don't know. He just said he needs to see you right away. He looks pretty frightened, if you ask me," Sheila added.

Mentally pushing aside the lingering cobwebs from his nightmare, he shook himself awake. The fever hadn't broken even though he had been sleeping all day.

After pulling on his robe, Trent walked downstairs and opened the front door. Standing before him was Captain Pullman, pointing a flashlight at the ground.

"Captain, what's going on?" Trent asked.

"Holloway, we need to talk, now," his captain replied.

"Now?" Holloway asked, a bit annoyed. But then he realized that his job sometimes had to come first.

Pullman didn't respond, and Holloway saw the serious expression on his captain's face in the bright moonlight.

"Why don't you come in while I finish getting dressed?"

"No, thanks. I'm fine right where I am," Pullman replied. "Come over to the van when you're ready. We'll talk in there."

Holloway hesitated. "Sure. Just give me a couple of minutes."

Holloway dressed quickly and grabbed his trench coat on the way out. He looked up the stairs at his wife and softly called to her. "Honey, I'm going outside. I'll be right back."

Captain Pullman motioned Holloway over to the van. He climbed in.

"Cigarette?" Pullman asked, shaking one loose from the pack.

"No, thanks. I'm trying to quit," Holloway replied.

As Trent watched Pullman shakily light his cigarette, he became nervous.

"Captain, with all due respect, what's wrong with you?"

"We have the fingerprint results back from the lab," Pullman said.

"And?" Holloway was wide awake now.

"The lab compared those found on the aquarium glass at the Evans scene to those found on the Dawson vehicle."

"So you want me to go with you to arrest the fucker?" Trent asked.

"No," Pullman sighed. "The prints belong to a dead man."

Holloway involuntarily shuddered. "How is that possible?"

Motionless in his seat, cigarette smoke swirling around him, Pullman said nothing.

"Captain."

"Yes?"

"How is that possible?"

"I don't know," Pullman replied. "But there's more. The skin samples found under Cassandra Evans' fingernails belong to the same dead man. The lab rechecked their work several times."

"Who's the man?" Holloway was almost too afraid to ask.

"James Brody. Do you remember him?"

Holloway searched his memory but came up blank. "Sorry, sir, can't say that I do."

"When you first started with the police force, what, fifteen, twenty years ago, we had just wrapped a case on James Brody. It was September and already cold, I remember. I had just made Administrative Sergeant, and my wife and I bought a house, the same one I just finished paying off." Pullman stopped and swallowed hard.

"Go on," Holloway gently urged.

"That autumn, we received a call about a drunk driver out near Route 10 in Rivershed who ran into a telephone pole. Three of us responded to the scene, and when we arrived, there was a man behind the wheel pinned under the crushed dashboard."

"Sounds nasty."

"Believe me, it was. But I found myself thinking there was something wrong with the scene. One, the guy wasn't drunk. Two, the weather conditions that night were fine. And three, the road was a dead end to begin with. I just didn't realize at the time how dead it really was." Pullman's three fingers were still in the air. He looked at them and grimaced. "But I found out soon enough, though."

"What happened, sir?" Holloway's interest in his captain's story grew by the second.

"We asked the man behind the wheel if he was okay, and he assured us that he was. But what bothered me about the whole thing was the way his face looked."

"What about it?" Holloway asked.

"His skin was the texture of leather and ruddy, like he had spent most of his life in the sun. And his eyes were so black I could see my reflection in them. He looked sharp and alert but not quite right," Pullman recalled.

"What happened next?"

"Well, we used the jaws of life to cut him out of the car. And once he was free, the paramedics pulled him out and put him on a stretcher. The fucking guy insisted that he was A-OK, but we insisted he go to the hospital. I don't think it registered with the other cops at the scene, but I knew right away that this guy wanted to leave the scene in one hell of a hurry. So I strolled over to where he was sitting on the stretcher. He asked me for a cigarette, and I gave him one."

"What was his name?" Holloway asked, knowing already what the Captain was going to say.

"He said his name was James Brody."

Pullman let that sink in for a moment and then continued, "I asked him how the accident had happened, and he said that he had fallen asleep at the wheel and woke up just before plowing into that telephone pole. I told him that I had seen that kind of thing happen many times before and to just be happy that he didn't get real banged up." Pullman paused to light another cigarette.

"I asked him what his business was up in Rivershed. He was driving with Delaware plates, you see. When he answered he said, 'Just business', I tried to get him to elaborate a bit and he finally loosened up."

"What did he say?" Holloway asked.

"Brody said 'I've come to seek out a great religion.'"

Holloway shifted in his seat. "That's the weirdest thing I ever heard."

"You're tellin' me. Though at the time, I thought nothing more of it. I fined him twenty dollars and let him go."

"What about the car?" Holloway asked.

"The car was towed to Briad's Junkyard. You should have seen it. It was literally wrapped around the telephone pole, crushed, completely totalled. At that time, I didn't know where James Brody lived, and I didn't really care. All I cared about was that he and his evil chiseled face leave Shallow Front."

"Three days later I got a call to go on down to Briad's. Apparently, something was really wrong. Christ, Vinny Briad could barely speak on the phone, but what he told me was enough to pique my interest, that's for sure," Pullman continued.

"And what happened when you went there?"

"Well, when I pulled into the lot, I immediately saw the look on Vinny's face. He was white as a ghost, and his expression, God, Trent, I'll never forget it."

"What did you find sir?" Holloway asked.

"I walked back behind the car lot and stopped because Vinny Briad wasn't following me."

" 'What's going on here?' I asked."

" 'Go see for yourself,' Vinny said."

" 'Ain't ya gonna show me?' I asked."

" 'Nope.' Vinny said. " 'Ain't no way you're gettin' me out back. The car is there just how we left it and everything that's in the trunk, we didn't touch.'"

"I knew it," Holloway said excitedly. "Drug dealer."

Pullman smiled sadly. "I wish, son. I only wish."

"What was it then?"

"As I walked closer to the trunk of the car, I saw something was worse than anything I seen in all my life." Pullman paused to light another cigarette. "A woman was stuffed in the trunk, laying in a pool of her own blood. Her mouth was stretched all the way open, and I remember wondering why I could see the fillings in her back teeth. Then I realized it was because her jaw had been broken and pried open."

"Jeez," Holloway gasped.

"Yeah. Well, it gets worse." Pullman shuddered at the memory. "This James Brody, the bastard who I let walk away, had cut the body into pieces. When the ME moved her, she sort of fell apart." Pullman took a deep drag on his cigarette and continued. "We found James Brody down in Briarwood two days later. He had murdered another victim and was trying to wash off the blood on his hands in a public fountain. An old woman phoned it in. He was caught red-handed. No pun intended."

"That was good, right?" Holloway asked.

"Well, yeah, it was good. Brody was tried and convicted and got the chair and all. But here we are, sitting in my van, talking about a dead man's fingerprints from a week-old crime scene."

As Pullman pulled out yet another cigarette, Holloway motioned for one. His captain lit it for him.

"Either we're looking for a murderer who has somehow managed to duplicate the fingerprints of a dead man, or like I said before, somebody made a mistake," Pullman concluded.

"I just don't see how that's possible," Holloway said. "Captain, where do we go from here?"

"I'm not sure myself, Detective, But I'll tell you one thing. This thing has got me scared enough to wake you up in the middle of the night."

"Thanks for filling me in, Captain. I gonna go now. I got a lot to think about."

"I understand. You coming into work tomorrow?"

"You mean today?" Holloway smiled.

Pullman looked at his watch. "Yeh, today."

"I'll be in at 9. I don't care how sick I feel."

"Good. See ya later then."

Holloway watched as the van pulled away then let himself back into his house. He never went back to sleep.

James Brody was not born in Shallow Front. He was pulled to it like a puppeteer's marionette.

Long before Trent Holloway had become a detective, James arrived to town, a drifter with nothing but a small suitcase filled with underwear, socks and several moderately clean shirts, and a guitar case. When he rented a short-term room in the center of town in one of the old apartment buildings, he wore an old brown suit jacket, jeans and scuffed black shoes. He was arrested in the same clothes.

When he was seven years old, his mother abandoned him and his father for a traveling salesman. She never said good-bye and James' father never explained. Instead, the elder Brody turned to God and pursued the path of the righteous and became a pastor, one very much like Pastor William Kline. James would not know Pastor Kline any better than he knew his own mother. Their paths would never cross.

James Brody's fate was never in his own hands. But he never knew it.

Pastor Brody spent countless hours praying in his study. As the years passed, James watched as the insanity grew in his father's eyes. The man believed that he had been cursed, that the devil was after him, that his wife walked out on him because he was evil. Nothing James said or did mattered. Pastor Brody believed he was possessed by evil.

Just after James turned twenty, his father killed himself with an axe. He didn't succumb to the horrible voices piercing his thoughts. Instead, he went into the barn, wedged his axe between the stumps of two downed trees and fell backwards onto the blade like a fallen angel.

James found his father's body two hours later and shortly after that, his head. His father's opened eyes were already half eaten by nature's scavengers. James screamed into the dead face, "Why?! Why Dad?!!" But any answer the dead eyes might have held would forever be unspoken.

He buried his father in the woods, not bothering to mark the grave. He grabbed the axe, ran into the house and hid it beneath the guitar in the case his mother had given him the last Christmas she was home. His father's bible and some clothes went into the suitcase. Then he left his childhood home forever.

Questions plagued James. Answers eluded him. Everywhere he went, he searched for the meaning of his life until one day he realized that the answers lie in religion. But not in one that he had known before but in a new religion. He searched in city after city and in town after town for the new religion. Slowly, like senility creeping in, he found his way. He kept the axe by his side to remind him of what could happen to him if he let his sorrow take hold. James did not believe in the devil but he was afraid of him none-the-less.

The revelation finally came.

James walked most of the time, on the shoulders of back roads and across open fields. He grew comfortable with his shadow and never felt alone.

One late summer afternoon, as the sun hung low in the sky silhouetting the delicate fingers of the cattails and field grass, a house appeared in front of him. It shimmered in the waning light like a mirage yet he was able to make out its details.

It was a very big house. Part of the slate roof had caved in and paint peeled like a snake shedding its skin. A grimy coat of dust and dirt fogged all of its windows. The front door was partially open. He could see that the wood had rotted from years of exposure to the elements.

The sun set just as he reached the porch. Low on the horizon, a full moon began to replace the sun. James waited until his eyes adjusted to the dark and approached the front door.

Why the fuck are you going into this house?

James felt a presence, and was certain that it had something to do with the new religion he yearned to find. He pushed down on the rusted latch and looked up at the door.

Welcome friends was scratched into the wood.

He entered the dark space. Through the gaping hole in the roof, moonglow illuminated the hallway enough for him to see the wide wooden planks of the floor and the ornate mahogany staircase. Standing in the foyer, he felt calm. He believed he had found what he had been looking for.

He took several steps into the house. The old floor felt sticky beneath his feet as if the rain and sun had melted the finish and dried it to a gummy consistency. When he looked down, however, rivulets of a dark liquid streaked the once pristine planks. Curious, he bent down and dipped his finger in the liquid. To his horror, the moonlight exposed it as blood, ruby red and freshly spilled.

Upon closer inspection, he noticed that the staircase in front of him was littered with the carcasses of dead rats. And lingering in the air was a smell that could burn the sanity right out of his mind, like a fire but more specific. The smell of books of matches that had recently been extinguished. Sulphur.

"This is the place..." James said out loud. "The place I've been looking for."

James gingerly walked up the stairs, kicking dead rats off the treads when they got in his way. Strangely, the smells of death and sulphur didn't deter him from discovering what waited for him at the top of the stairs.

The stair posts jutted at odd angles and many were cracked and broken. Paintings lined the wall to his left and covered the wall at the top of the stairs. They came into view suddenly as if emerging from a dream. They depicted scenes of young men and women being burned alive and of children being ripped apart by wolves beneath a wooden cross that was engulfed in flames. It dawned on James that he was looking at scenes from hell.

He lost all track of time in the house that was the embodiment of evil. He felt it as acutely as he felt the dampness of the evening creep into his bones.

In the dim moonlight, a voice entered his mind. *I hold the leash,* it said. *You hear me, motherfucker? I said I hold the leash. Pay attention!*

A long hallway adjacent to the staircase led to several closed doors. James started down the hall to his right but a loud, piercing voice stopped him dead in his tracks.

"James, this place has been waiting for you for years. Welcome. The windows will protect you from the outside world, and the doors won't open once closed, but the things inside here are alive and well. Your people got it all so wrong. There is no pit of fire, no creatures of flame, no eternity of heat. There is only damnation. You know about that, don't you James?"

"Who's here? Who are you?" James screamed.

Who do you think it is, James?

"Jesus? Is that you?" James asked excitedly. Who else but Jesus could have spoken to him? Had he not been looking for salvation in a new religion? Hadn't he been drawn to this old house after years of searching? James fell to his knees and started to pray.

Then came the laughter, high-pitched and insane. Madness rang out and into James Brody's ears. He heard evil in the laughter and scrambled to his feet, ready to run down the stairs and out the door. But his feet wouldn't move. The laughter subsided as one of the doors opened to him. A brilliant beam of moonlight pierced the darkness just like in the old religious paintings he had seen in hundreds of churches during his travels.

"Jesus isn't the answer you seek, James," the voice said.

James entered the room.

The door closed behind him as soon as he entered the very large room. Moonlight filtered through the dirty windows and James was able to see paintings on the walls. Hundreds of them hung haphazardly, in all shapes and sizes. He inspected those nearest to him and staggered backwards when he realized their subject matter. All were scenes from his life.

In fright, he took a step backwards and tripped and fell on the rug. He landed eye to eye with a head, a human head. The rug was made out of a human being. It had been skinned and stretched just like a bear. The eyes were two black porcelain globes that stared lifelessly at James, and its mouth was stretched open wide as if it had been preserved in mid-scream.

The mouth began to move.

"Hello, James," it said.

James rolled off the rug and shrieked. He ran for the door.

"Don't be afraid, preacher's son," the face said.

James heard a clapping sound and turned to see where it was coming from. The rug was bringing its hands together and clapping them in applause. The disjointed arms flapped loosely over the creature's head.

James shrieked. "No! NO!!!!!" He turned to reach for the doorknob but the door swung open before him.

"Wonderful!" the voice bellowed.

James could not see its source but the voice was very near and he was very frightened.

"How do you like my home?" the voice asked.

"GET ME OUT OF HERE!" James screamed. "OH DEAR CHRIST LET ME OUT!"

"And go where?" the voice asked in a disconcerting calm and inquisitive way. "Where did you want to go, James?"

James looked back at the body on the floor and shook his head. The rug was a bear after all. And the paintings on the walls were actually antlers of varying shapes and sizes.

"Why don't you come over here?" the voice coaxed.

Suddenly, James bolted for the door. He needed his

axe.

"You left it at the top of the stairs," the voice reminded him. "Did you forget already?"

James froze in place. It was impossible that his thoughts could be read yet the voice knew exactly what he had been thinking.

From the shadows in front of James, an old man appeared like a ghost. He wore an old moth-eaten suit and a cowboy hat. Long slender fingers gripped an old pocketwatch. He flipped it open and checked the time.

"My, my," the man whispered. "Time's running short my friend." He glanced up at James. "Yes, I am your friend," he said.

James listened and glanced up at the ceiling.

"Not his friend, James. Mine." The man smiled and pointed to the Bible in James' hand.

James dropped the Bible as if it was burning his hands. When it hit the floor, the loud thud it made resounded throughout the huge space and brought him back to reality.

The man had taken a step closer into the dead light of the moon. His head had transformed into a goat's, its horns curled back from his forehead and its wild eyes glowed red.

James found the door knob just as it opened its grotesque mouth. Long twisted teeth lined its black gums.

"You no longer need to run, my lad. Just bring me a face, a face I can wear," the thing said.

"What are you talking about!" James screamed through hot tears.

"Are you deaf, James? I need a FACE!" the thing bellowed.

James ran in the dim light, fumbled the staircase but found the wooden handle of his axe.

He stood still for a moment, willing his breathing to return to normal, stared into the darkness and waited for the thing to come running after him. Then he smelled a familiar odor. Burning matches.

"Where are you running to Jamesy James? Are you going to run around town with that thing?"

James shook from head to toe.

"Why did you come here, preacher boy?"

"I...I didn't," James said. "I'm dreaming this."

"Perhaps," the terrible voice taunted. "And perhaps when I come for you and all those pretty young girls who are no longer pure, you'll know that this was no dream. And when you help me of your own free will, you'll believe in me. So do yourself a favor, Jamesy, broaden my path. Pave the way for me."

James stepped forward. "I'll send you to hell first!"

"James," the thing spoke, "this is hell."

An object rolled down the hall and stopped at James' leg. He slowly looked down and saw his father's head. The thing howled in laughter and the room ignited.

"That's right, James. You're in hell, the real deal. Hell is not a pit way, way down beneath the surface. It is here. In my house," the demon said. "I hold the leash to all your lives. I paint the pictures. I make the days begin and the nights end. You understand me, daddy killer?"

James could hardly breathe.

"That's right, James. You killed daddy with that axe."

"No," James said as he shook his head. "No, it's a lie. THE DEVILS LIES!"

"Do I? Well, say what you will, but you know it's true. I am your friend. I have always been there for you. I was there when you needed help with Daddy, don't you remember? We are friends for life and beyond, James. Till death do us part, just like in marriage."

In horror, James fell to his knees, tears ran down his cheeks.

"I...I killed daddy?" he asked.

"Don't think of it like that, James. Think of it as you liberated yourself from an extremely destructive environment. Think of our discussion as one of those you have with those shrinks you always go see. I'm here to help set you free from your troubles just like you did for your father. No charge."

"I set him..fr..free?"

"Yes you did. That's right. You set him free from all those years of abuse, and now I want you to do the same for me. Until I find a face I can use, I want you to walk the streets and take what is yours. Kill the damned for they are sinners."

James shook his head. "You mean broaden your path."

"Yes, that's exactly what I mean." They both looked at the gleaming axe blade.

"So, what do you say, buddy boy?" the devil asked. "I can take anybody I want and I chose you, Jamesy James..."

I hold the leash...

Rivershed is a small section of Spring Garden. All was quiet on Main Street at 7 in the morning as Jessica Frommel unlocked the door of her parents' thrift shop, Frommel's Things, and turned on the lights. The little chimes on the door jingled as she shut and locked it behind her.

Most days, Jessica arrived at the shop at 8:30. Her routine was to enjoy a few minutes of her favorite music while checking the previous day's register receipts. But today, she needed some extra time to herself.

Jessica opened her purse and grabbed the slim package inside. She walked to the back of the shop to the bathroom, flicked on the switch and closed the door behind her.

Jessica knew that she had made a few mistakes in her nineteen years. What kid doesn't? But it was difficult when your parents expected so much from you and you had to hide the reality of who you were. Fat from sneaking too much junk food, lonely, pretending your friends really were friends, not just kids who teased you. Mistakes you could never tell anyone about.

Like the big mistake she made in believing that Scott Cheswald told her the truth while she laid naked on his basement couch.

"Are you wearing protection, baby?" she had asked.

"Damn straight. I play it safe," he had assured her.

She slipped the box out of the plain brown paper bag and prepared Scott for his lie detector test.

As she sat in the antiseptic whiteness of the small bathroom waiting for the results, the feeling of fear that had plagued her since she bought the test kit dwindled a bit. *I am unique and strong and I'll be just fine,* she tried to convince herself. Then she stared down at the white plastic test strip and her fear burst wide open again.

A pink plus sign. Pregnant. She wanted to scream.

With her mismatched eyes, one blue and one green, she saw her future, and it was wrapped in a diaper.

"I told you to stay away from him, Jess!" her mother would remind her.

"Damn it! Just look at my pregnant daughter. Another mess. Another mess! You're just in another mess..." her father would cry.

How could she tell her parents when all they would say is, 'another mess'? How could she look up at her mother with the same one-blue, one-green eyes? They would glare at her. How could she face her father who would rock back and forth in his rocking chair holding his head in his hands?

"Why angel? Why did you do this? A baby? Why? You had your whole life in front of you," they would say.

The bell above the front door chimed.

"What the hell?" Jessica said, startled by the bell. Someone was in the store. *But how? I locked the front door.*

Before her fear had a chance to grow, she realized that one or both of her parents must have decided to come in early.

But then again, she thought, *they would have seen my car outside and would have said something by now.*

"WHO IS IT?!" Jessica cried out from behind the bathroom door. She stood, pulled her pants up hastily and stepped out of the bathroom. Only a heavy silence filled the empty shop.

And the lights were off.

"What the hell?" Jessica whispered to herself.

"I hope you're not in another mess, Jessica Anne Frommel."

The hair on her arms and the back of her neck stood up straight as goose bumps coursed over her body. The voice was male but so low, it sounded more like a breeze. *How does he know my name? Who is it?*

Jessica inched her way towards the light switch. But in her head, she heard her mother scream, "Fuck the lights! You need the phone!"

All Jessica could think of was, *How am I gonna tell my parents?*

And in a voice more sinister than anything she could have imagined, she had her answer.

"You don't have to."

Jessica stopped dead in her tracks. The voice sounded like a shift in the air from the now wide open front door. It sounded like it was coming from a very old man with sand in his throat.

"Quite a mess you're in, Jess," he said, closer this time, almost as if he was inside her head.

"Who...who is that?" was all Jessica could think to say before reason took hold, and she turned to run to the back door.

She didn't get far.

Standing before her in the back doorway, silhouetted by the brilliant early morning sun, was a tall figure. Jessica's right leg suddenly stiffened as her muscles seized up in pure terror. Her heart skipped a beat then jumped into her throat.

"Wha...I mean...who...are...what?" Jessica couldn't see so she held up her hand to the blinding sun that spilled from behind the dark figure. Her eyes adjusted, and she was able to see a man dressed entirely in black and wearing a cowboy hat that shadowed his face. She couldn't see his eyes but she was able to see his mouth.

He smiled.

"Oh my God!" Jessica screamed.

"God abandoned you, my dear," the man said, "a long time ago."

Jessica knew she had to get out of there as fast as she could, but her legs wouldn't move.

"Tell me your name," the voice commanded.

Jessica never had the chance to answer. The man who had torn out Cassandra Evans' throat and who had ripped Amanda Dawson apart snapped Jessica Frommel's neck with ease. He smiled at the sharp cracking sound.

Jessica fell to the ground in a lifeless heap. Then in a skilled quickness no being on earth could possess, he ripped the clothing from her body. The smell of burning matches filled the air.

Two hours later, Kimberly Frommel arrived at her shop expecting to find Jessica. Instead, she found the front door wide open, the lights off, and a pregnancy test strip on the floor. She immediately called the police.

Officer Mike Walker arrived first at Frommel's Things

and found Kimberly and Walter Frommel in a frenzy. Detective Holloway arrived shortly thereafter.

Alex Wechter was riding his bicycle to his friend's house on an old dirt road. It was a bumpy ride. *They are never gonna pave this dead old road,* he thought to himself even though he always wished they would. But Alex understood that some things were more important than others. Living things needed more attention than those things that were dead.

So in a strange way, it was only appropriate that Alex would prove himself wrong.

As he passed a grassy ditch, something caught his eye. He double-backed and when he got closer, slammed down on the brakes of his ten speed. He slid sideways to a stop.

Lying face up not ten feet from where he stopped breathing was the nude body of the girl from the thrift shop.

Holloway got to work very much before nine. The night without sleep didn't end so he didn't have to wake up to his alarm clock. He just got dressed in his work clothes after Pullman left and drove downtown to his office. He watched the sun rise out his window.

Trent was five, as old as his own son is now, when his mother died of a brain tumor. The unknown tumor had ruptured at the State Fair and drowned his mother's last coherent thoughts. It took Trent ten years to get over it.

As a child, he thought a lot about becoming a doctor so he could cure brain tumors in all mothers everywhere and save their children from the utter grief he suffered. But instead, he decided to join the military.

Trent and his father, Harold Holloway, continued to live in the same house after Mary died. The reminders that his mother had actually once existed were constant. More and more over the course of time, the little touches she left behind comforted him. But it wasn't so for his father. Trent watched what he now understood was his father's deterioration. But as a child, he didn't understand.

While they were married, Harold never drank alcohol. As a younger man, he had visited the bottom of the bottle many times and knew what things could come slithering up. But as a married man and father, he did the right thing, maintained a job and took care of his family. But since his wife was dead, he couldn't think of a reason not to drink. Trent witnessed the birth of the monster inside his father and unwittingly nurtured it to maturity until it ran rampant like the serial killer in Shallow Front.

The first time Harold Holloway ever laid a hand on his son was after a football game. Trent was fifteen.

In the fall of that unforgettable year, Harold came to watch Trent play. He rarely went anywhere but had chosen a soggy October day to make his appearance on the field.

It had been raining hard for hours, and the field was

one large puddle.

The play was decided in the huddle, and Trent was to go long for the touchdown. After the snap, he ran with all his might. He had seen his father in the stands and knew how much it would mean to him if he caught the ball and scored. Winning was paramount to his father. Win at all costs. Do whatever it took.

Trent reached the end zone well before any of the opposing players. He stood waiting for the ball to catch up to him. He had all the time in the world.

It came a second later, straight at him, spiraling beautifully into his hands. And he dropped it. The slick ball slipped out of his hands. Trent felt the cold grip of embarrassment and humiliation as the ball tumbled out of reach. He felt his father's eyes boring into him from the stands.

After the game, Harold waited in the old pick-up truck for Trent, just outside the locker room. Trent did not shower. He changed his clothes and walked out of the school. Tears slid down his face with each step he took.

I shouldn't have missed that pass. Such an easy pass. He's gonna kill me, he thought.

It took all his strength to walk up to the pickup truck to where his father waited, staring out the windshield, rigid, his hair as black as midnight slicked back, his leather jacket soaked through.

"Hello, father," Trent said tentatively.

Harold did not reply as he put the truck in drive and headed home.

Trent saw the disappointment in his father's eyes. It glowed in them so brightly, he knew he would never forget.

"How the hell could you miss that toss, son?" Harold asked, still looking straight ahead.

"I tried my be-"

"HOW THE FUCK COULD YOU LET THAT BALL SLIP THROUGH YOUR FINGERS??!" his father screamed.

Trent couldn't answer and simply lowered his gaze to his father's black, chrome-tipped cowboy boots.

As his father reached under the seat for the flask of whiskey he kept there, Trent saw the anger inside his father boil away the dampness on his clothes and skin.

"Sorry, but Trent...you need to practice. You need to pray. And by God, you need to move on," his father said and then slugged him with the back of his right fist.

From that moment on, his father abused him daily for several years. It wasn't always physical abuse. Many times he simply berated Trent until the boy became numb. For years, Trent blamed himself. And even though his father was the real one to blame, Trent couldn't see it. So, he punished himself by taking up cigarettes at seventeen.

Trent knew that if his father ever found out that he was smoking, he would be beaten. He would yank Trent's hair out of his scalp, causing the skin to bleed again. He would use the belt on him and raise again the welts that had finally healed. In some morbid way, Trent wanted his father to find out so he would finally be beaten to death and it would be over.

Harold Holloway grew more insane each year, and his

son was to blame. For the house being repossessed by the tax collectors. For giving him cancer. Of course he didn't get it from working in the asbestos factory all those years. Trent gave it to him.

When Harold finally did catch Trent smoking cigarettes, he beat his son within a centimeter of his life. With a 2x4, the elder Holloway connected with Trent's ribs over and over again so hard that the wood split in two. Trent pissed blood for a week. His excuse to the nurses at the hospital was that he fell down the stairs. He told his Aunt Florence that he fell off his motorcycle.

When Trent turned nineteen, he enlisted in the army.

At his first meeting with his recruiting officer, he showed up with fresh bruises on his face. He told Sergeant Bryant from Fort Worthington that he had been in a scuffle at an after hours club. Luckily, Sergeant Bryant wasn't born yesterday and took special care with his new, young recruit.

Harold Holloway learned that his only child was joining the military from Aunt Flo. Trent hadn't seen or spoken to his father since the 2x4 incident two years earlier and didn't care to. He instead preferred to remember the father he used to love, the one who took him fishing and to Carson Park to play catch. The father who used to whisk the family down to the Delaware beaches. The one who used to tuck him into bed each night.

Harold Holloway died of alcohol poisoning while Trent was in basic training.

Trent felt the old feelings as fresh as when he first felt them. *When will I not?* he asked himself as he turned from his office window. *Dear Old Dad.*

Later that afternoon, Frank Lion knocked on Darla Goodman's door.

"Well, well, well. How are you, Officer?" Darla asked with a playful smile at the corners of her lips.

"Not bad, Darla," his response accompanied a long, lingering look into her eyes.

"Been a while, Lion. Wanna come in?" she asked then licked her lips. Frank Lion forgot all about his wife.

"Sure do, Darla."

He grabbed her by the arms and pulled her close to him. Darla took a step back and dragged him inside with her. They kissed long and hard and then disappeared behind the closed door.

After their tumble, Detective Lion watched the news with his mistress. He was mostly naked, wearing just his t-shirt, and held Darla in his arms. Channel 6 was covering the Dawson and Evans cases again.

Photos of the women both before and after their deaths had been displayed on-screen so many times already that they had somehow lost their meaning. But Lion would never forget the smell at each of their murder scenes. Nor would he forget the horror of what had been done to those pretty, young, pregnant women. He felt angry and helpless as never before.

"Why would a person do that?" Darla asked as she laid her head in his lap.

"I don't know. This is a strange town, always has been."

"Do you think your guys will catch this lunatic?"

Frank puffed on his cigar. "You betcha."

It had started to rain. The windows of the third precinct were almost opaque with condensation and fog.

Detective Jeremy Harris walked down the marble steps of the justice department next door to the municipal building. He saw Detective Holloway next to the newspaper stand paying for a cup of coffee.

"And let there be tigers," Harris said. Holloway turned and smiled.

"What brings you up here?" Harris asked.

"I was researching the old files about the deceased James Brody."

Harris paid for his own coffee and smiled. He stirred in the non-dairy creamer and a packet of sugar and took a sip.

"Trent, I gotta tell you. I am really perplexed over Billy Warrington committing suicide."

"Yeah, I know. It's been keeping me up nights, I can tell you that," Holloway agreed.

"Why would someone do that? Right in front of everyone?"

"I don't know. Listen, there's a lot of shit going on here I don't understand at all," Holloway said.

"You mean the fingerprints?"

"You heard about that," Holloway started. "What do you think? I mean, we can't very well assume a dead man is doing all this, can we?"

"No, that would be pretty fucking unbelievable. And I think Pullman would have you committed over it," Harris chuckled.

"James Brody has been dead and buried for years. It isn't possible that our psycho is using his prints, is it?

Where would he get them. Why would he even think to get 'em?"

"I don't know. I think Pullman and the rest of the crime lab are beating a dead horse with all of this," Harris said.

"No pun intended?" Holloway asked then added seriously, "Well, I wake up every day hoping that it is over because I don't have a clue as to how it's going to end."

"It never will end. All you'll ever have is a box of clues leading to nothing. I have a feeling that this door is going to remain locked. We got what? Two murders, similar but not all that much alike. And a hundred unanswered questions."

Holloway thought Harris just might be right.

Suddenly, a cell phone blared. Both men checked their pockets. It was Holloway's.

Trent listened intently to the voice on the other end of the phone then ended the call without saying a word. He looked up at Detective Harris. His eyes said it all. Something was very wrong. Holloway put the phone back in his pocket.

"They found another one, didn't they?" Harris asked. A rush of cool horror swelled in his temples. He looked at his steaming coffee and threw it in the trash. "Oh God."

Both detectives raced to their cars.

Jessica Frommell was pronounced dead on the scene by the coroner. The ambulance crew arrived, and after the scene was photographed and the evidence had been gathered, they zipped up Jessica's body in a black plastic bag and took her away. There was nothing more they could do. The body of another pregnant woman was ditched on the side of Creek Road, an unpaved back stretch through the Pine Valley Condominiums. A hysterical little boy riding his bike to his friend's house had discovered her.

She was found unlike the others. Amanda Dawson had been disemboweled. Cassandra Evans had been raped, molested, strangled, and bitten to death. Jessica was found naked, laying in a twisted mass of cattails. Her neck was broken.

"You think it's the same guy?" Harris asked.

Holloway stood motionless and looked around the crime scene. There had been a passing shower earlier in the morning and the grass was still damp. The flies buzzed around the area, looking for the meal that had been taken away.

"I know it is," Holloway said with conviction as he bent down and plucked pieces of grass with his gloved hands and placed them in evidence bags. "In fact, I think he's watching us right now."

He likes to watch.

Frank Lion's unmarked car pulled up on the other side of the road. He got out of the car with a spring in his step. The medical examiner had just arrived.

My wife better never know what I've been up to. But I can't help it. Darla is good to me, Frank thought.

"Well, I guess that makes three now," Detective Lion said, taking a long pull on his cigar.

"You think its the same guy, Frank?" Jeremy Harris asked.

"You mean you can't smell it?" Frank looked at the

other detectives quizzically. "Who else could it be?"

"But Frank," Holloway asked, "where's it coming from?"

"I smell it, too. It smells like matches. But so?" Detective Harris commented more interested in the victim than the vague smell of matches.

"Her neck," Harris continued. "Her neck was bruised all the way around. If it was our boy, he doesn't seem particularly married to any one style of killing. The first two were pretty bruised up, contusions and all. Dawson was disemboweled, for chrissakes. But this time, he removed the victim from the scene and brought her here." To everyone's surprise, Harris seemed to be really tuned in and turned on.

"Good point, Harris," Lion said.

"And you know what else?" Detective Harris continued, rubbing his blonde goatee thoughtfully.

"What?"

"Where are the tire tracks? Where are the shoe prints? All we have are sneaker prints from the kid who found her."

"Well, gentlemen, that's why we're detectives. Let's wrap this up and catch the son of a bitch," Lion declared, obviously anxious to get back to what he had been doing.

"Who's gonna tell her folks?" Holloway asked.

"I've got Officer Squall over at the thrift shop right now," Lion said.

Holloway followed the ME back to the office this time, following him down that stretch of hallway once again, wondering how many more times he would have to before it was finished.

"You know, Detective Holloway, this is becoming an obsession for whoever's doing it," Derrick Moore stated as he slipped his fingers into the thin rubber gloves. "I don't see anything unusual on the grass you pulled up, but we will run the same tests as before. I see much more semen this time and more severe vaginal hemorrhaging, however. And in this case, the perpetrator spun her head around on her shoulders like a top. Not only is her neck broken in multiple places but so are her clavicals."

"She was raped?" Holloway asked.

"Oh, most definitely," Derrick Moore replied.

"Doctor Moore, I've been meaning to ask you something. At the first two crime scenes, we smelled sulphur, like burning matches. And then at this third scene, even though we were outside and a wind had kicked up, we could still smell it."

"Sulphur?" Moore asked skeptically.

"Yes, like burning matches. What is that from?"

"I couldn't say," Moore confessed. "I hadn't noticed the smell of sulphur when I performed the two autopsies."

Holloway stood to the left as the team of examiners lifted the body bag onto the steel table. They unzipped it and several flies escaped from the warm blackness into the light.

As Holloway watched the flies fly away, it suddenly dawned on him, as it had for Harris, that the madman was never going to stop.

"Now let's see what we've got, shall we?" Derrick Moore said a little to cheerily for Trent.

"Caucasian. Female. Identity, Jessica Anne Frommel,

age nineteen, no distinguishing marks, red hair. The color of her eyes are..." *Who will paint for me?* Derrick Moore stopped mid-sentence.

Holloway straightened up and approached the table. "What's the matter? What's wrong, Dr. Moore?"

"Oh...my...God," Moore stammered. "Detective, please come closer. You're not going to believe this."

Holloway approached the table and underneath the fluorescence, peered at what the good doctor wanted him to see.

The color drained from the detective's face.

Not much got to Holloway. He was a detective who had been to many murder scenes, a detective who had witnessed a man commit suicide with a shotgun, a detective who saved a young girl from drowning by performing CPR on her, a detective who shot and killed a renowned drug dealer from New York's Mafia syndicate.

Detective Trent Holloway had been through a lot, had seen a lot. But never anything like this.

With an eerie precision even Holloway's untrained eye could discern, someone had carved Jessica Frommel's eyes from her skull. A single tear of blood ran from the corner of the victim's empty right eye socket as Dr. Moore moved her head.

In the place of her eyes were two porcelain globes, both white and glossy.

"I can't believe this," Derrick Moore said, truly incredulous.

"No, I can't either. How did this guy do it?" Holloway asked.

"Well, I can't say exactly. But whoever did it has a

knowledge of anatomy and the skill of a surgeon. And, Detective, if I were you, I'd be looking for a man with very large hands."

"Why do you say that?"

"Well, see how her neck is broken? A normal injury to the spine will either dislodge the vertebrae or separate them, causing bone fractures that usually lead to death."

"Okay."

Both men looked once more into the porcelain eyes of the dead woman, knowing that the road ahead of them was growing ever longer and without warning signs.

It begins.

Holloway knew this was just the beginning, and if something wasn't done fast, it would go on forever. He was doing everything he could. The State Police had issued an APB and made capture a priority. The fingerprints found on Ms. Frommel's purse were fed through Interpol. If they were indeed James Brody's, it would come as no surprise. But what good would knowing where the prints came from if the man was long dead?

The only other clue Holloway had to work with was the smell of burning matches. *Why did the crime scenes smell of sulphur?*

James Brody's body was exhumed two days later, if for no other reason than to prove that he was indeed still in his coffin. Perhaps enough of his decomposed body would remain to gather DNA evidence as well.

Inside the police forensics lab, Holloway stood by while Dr. Moore's assistants pried open the lid of the coffin.

The wood had become so brittle, opening it sounded like stepping on dry twigs.

As they struggled with the coffin, Dr. Moore said, "I don't know what you expect to find, Detective, once we get this lid off."

Trent remained calm. "Just open it. We'll know once we're inside."

The lid finally popped off. They lifted it and placed it top down on an adjacent table.

Holloway watched.

The odor emanating from the dark chamber of the coffin was putrid. But the other smell, that of recently extinguished matches, was equally as horrific.

Alright, Holloway thought, *Now, I'm really afraid.*

The smell of decay and death swirled up and out of the coffin. The rotted corpse lay with hands crossed across a decomposing blue suit jacket. The hair was long and dusty gray. Holloway was amazed to learn that hair continues to grow after death. The first time he saw an exhumed body, he was startled, to say the least.

"Do you smell that smell I told you about, Doctor?"

Doctor Moore held his hand over his nose. "Yes...yes, I do. It smells like sulphur."

"Then please explain to me, sir, why we can smell it at all the crime scenes? And even more importantly, why can we smell it now?"

Moore looked at Holloway. "I can't answer you, Detective."

"WHY THE FUCK NOT?" Holloway yelled in frustration.

"Because I don't know," Doctor Moore replied with deep resentment.

The silence that followed was filled with tension.

"And truthfully, Detective, I don't want to know," Moore admitted.

"Ever since Cassandra Evans and Amanda Dawson were found murdered, the town hasn't been the same. And I don't believe that the Bill Warrington suicide isn't part of the equation either," he concluded.

"Bullshit!" Holloway spat. "Bill Warrington was a bad seed. At first I suspected that he might have been the murderer. But now that there's a third victim, and he's dead..." Holloway didn't need to finish his thoughts.

"I'm sorry I yelled at you, Doctor," Holloway apologized.

"No problem," Doctor Moore calmly replied.

The DNA of the seminal fluid found in Jessica Frommel did not match the DNA of the deceased James Brody. As slim as it was, Holloway finally had a real clue with which to proceed, not just phantom odors and dead men's fingerprints. It gave him some hope of solving the crimes. Unfortunately, things did not get any better. They only got worse.

On Saturday morning, the week after Jessica was found, Holloway was once again sitting in his office. Agent Summers, head of the FBI crime lab in Capitol Hill, was on the phone. The prints had been run through the computer and the results were in. The four fingerprints found on Jessica Frommell's bloody purse all had different sworl patterns, and all four prints belonged to four very different, very peculiar, very unique and very dead people.

"What!" Holloway exclaimed. "Who are they?"

"Timothy Waltz. Dead at age fifty, heart problems. He had one last and ultimately fatal heart attack six years ago. His wife found him on the floor by the bed."

"I don't under..."

Agent Summers continued, "Another belongs to a Hell's Angel who was killed in Widigo, just outside Kansas City. He was shot mob-style, behind the head, almost ten years ago."

"Jesus Christ," Holloway heard himself say.

"Yeah, that's just what I said. I don't understand either. Just like the semen sample from the second murder. It matches what we found in the Evans woman, same DNA pattern and all, but we have no one to compare it to. And we certainly can't keep exhuming dead people. That would be absurd."

Holloway thought for a moment then decided to ask anyway. Heck, what's a little embarrassment if you could solve several brutal murders? "Would it?" finally escaped his lips.

Agent Summers didn't respond right away. All Holloway could hear on the other end of the line was his rhythmic breathing.

After a long ten seconds, Summers responded, "That's a bit, you know, ridiculous."

"I know, I know. I guess...oh, just forget I said anything." Then Holloway added, "We've already made comparisons to James Brody but no dice."

"Well, I understand why you asked. This is the weirdest case I've seen, ever. It gives me the damn creeps," Summers said. "There are a lot of smart criminals out there. But I've never heard of one who could replicate fingerprints of the dead."

"Who were the other two?" Holloway asked.

Agent Summers got back on track. "Simon Harvis from Duchester. He was a well-known wine maker. And finally, Charles Bomon. He was a bum, as far as we know."

"I just don't get it," Holloway said.

"Yeah, it has my brain twisted up in a knot, that's for sure. All four of these people have been dead for at least ten years."

Holloway took a long swallow of water from the glass. His fever was lifting slightly.

"Well, thank you, sir. Will you fax all this over?"

"I'll take care of it right away," Agent Summers replied and hung up.

Holloway felt achy but better. He loosened his tie, trying to convince himself that it was the fever that made his throat feel constricted. But he knew better.

In front of him were two photos of Jessica Frommel. One was a black and white crime scene photo and the other was her color high school graduation photo. Jessica had two distinctly different eye colors, just like her mother.

Then Sergeant Jeremy Harris screamed.

Detective Harris was in his cubicle, twenty feet away from Holloways' office, close to the hallway and Captain Pullman's office. The squad room was as busy as ever, all the top dogs were driving themselves crazy over the pregnancy murders. Every patrolman was on heavy watch, the swinging pendulum of fear showed in their eyes. What would they do if they found another victim? How would they feel if one of their wives became pregnant?

And how did this madman know that the women were pregnant? What was his motive? Holloway had already confirmed with Dr. Moore that there was no possible way of knowing that all three women were pregnant and concluded that it must be coincidence. Holloway wasn't convinced.

The pendulum of fear swung fast and hard, dropping in heavy sweeps. The community whispered among itself and slept under a blanket of dark clouds. All three towns were affected — Garrison City, Shallow Front and Spring Garden. The evil that had descended upon them was merciless and unnerving, and no end was in sight.

Jeremy Harris had arrested two men on drug charges and was filling out his report as the dealers waited in one of the many holding cells. A bustle of people came in and out of the station house, mostly police, some criminals.

"Detective," Heather Mills interrupted Harris. He looked up from his keyboard and barely saw her eyes above the large box she was carrying.

"Here, let me help you," Harris said as he got up to take the package from Heather.

"What do you think it is?" she asked. "Maybe you have a secret admirer."

"Someone likes me? Will wonders never cease," he smiled. "Probably a gift from my girlfriend for my birthday."

"Oh, Happy Birthday! I didn't know or else we would have thrown you a party," Heather said sarcastically.

He ignored her and said, "Let's just put this on the desk." He cleared an area and sat the box down.

It was cumbersome but not heavy. It was about two and a half feet tall and twelve inches square.

"Ain't ya gonna open it?" Heather insisted with her hands on her hips.

It didn't take Jeremy Harris long to tear the silver wrapping paper off the box. "I wonder what she got me," he mumbled.

Under the wrapping was a plain cardboard box. Harris used his pen knife to slash the packing tape down the long side of the box. Inside, he found an oblong shape protected in bubble wrap. Detective Harris, who should have known better, pulled the object from the box and slipped off the wrap.

"What the...?" Harris started.

A sheet of white paper fell to his desk as he uncovered his gift. It was a white ceramic angel, shiny and expensive-looking, about two feet tall. Its hands were together in prayer at its waist and its head was oversized in comparison to its body.

Detective Harris noticed the sheet of paper and picked it up. It was folded once in half. He opened it up and read it.

Do you see what eye see?

Detective Harris' hand fell as if in slow motion as his eyes came to rest on the face of the angel. Its eyes were human. One green, one blue.

That's when he screamed. Detective Holloway bolted

from his chair and went to investigate. Of the eleven cops in the station, all but the desk officer drew their guns and ran to Harris' cubicle. Heather was pushed aside and rebelled. "I want to see what it is!" she cried.

Captain Pullman ran from his office as well. He was unable to see past the mass of cops and ordered them to stand aside.

"What's going on here?" he demanded.

"I brought him his birthday present and..." Heather began.

"Heather," Pullman interrupted, "Please go back to your desk." She pouted but did as she was told.

With no other distractions, Pullman saw what the commotion was all about. "What the hell do we have here?" he asked.

Holloway had just finished examining the angel and explained. "Someone has a very sick sense of humor. The eyes in this statue's face belong to Jessica Frommel."

"What? Am I hearing you right, Holloway?" Pullman asked.

"Yes. Yesterday at the ME's, I watched as Dr. Moore pulled porcelain eyes from the sockets of the victim. Jessica's own eyes were missing." Using a paper clip, Holloway carefully slid the note closer, careful not to damage any fingerprint evidence.

"Get some gloves," Pullman said in a low voice. He then addressed Harris. "Harris, what the hell did you think you were doing opening a box in the squad room? There could have been a bomb in there, for chrissakes!" Pullman shook his head in disbelief.

"Show's over folks. Get back to work. Everything is

under control," Holloway said as he tried to block the view into Harris' cubicle.

Detective Freeburgh, who witnessed the entire scene, stepped in and assisted. "That's right, folks. We got it covered here."

"Thanks, cowboy," Holloway said.

"No problem, man," Freeburgh replied as he shooed away the last of the bystanders.

"Oh...holy shit..." Harris mumbled. He was still shaking. His throat was dry, and he couldn't swallow.

"Jeremy, where did the box come from?" Holloway asked.

"He-Hea-Heather gave it to me," he stammered.

"HEATHER!" Pullman yelled. Heather Mills came running.

"Yes, sir?"

"Where did you get this damn thing? Don't look at it! Where did you get the box, the gift?" he demanded.

"It was in the mailroom, in the clerk's bin. Just sitting there this morning when I came. Addressed to Detective Harris...Detective Jeremy Harris," she corrected herself.

Pullman looked at Holloway. "Alright, no one else touch anything, and I mean no one. Holloway, have every inch of this thing dusted for prints. The note, too. And Harris!"

"Yes, sir?" Harris looked up.

"Go outside, get some fresh air. I want you to take a break," Pullman ordered.

"Thank you, sir," Harris replied. He tried to walk away from his desk, but found it difficult to take the first step. His fear had him glued to the floor.

"Holloway," Pullman said.

"Yes, Captain."

"I want you to stick around. After we dust this thing, I want you to take it to the chem lab. Then I want blood and DNA tests done. I wanna be goddamned sure those eyes belong to John Doe's latest victim."

"Sure thing, Captain," Holloway replied.

Holloway fast-tracked the results from the lab and by the next afternoon, he had answers to several of his questions. The angel itself contained nothing else — no more notes, no bomb, no other body parts. The eyes recovered did indeed belong to Jessica Frommel. The fingerprints from the note belonged to yet another dead man, Willie Zigs. But there were no other prints found anywhere on the box or wrapping paper. And Jessica Frommel had been pregnant when she was murdered.

Do you see what eye see?

Mike Tulk, a reporter for the Garrison Herald Tribune, covered the story:

> Police have released the name of the third victim of the Shallow Front Serial Killer. Jessica Frommel, age nineteen and co-owner of the thrift shop known as Frommel's Things in Spring Garden, was identified by her parents at the county morgue. Jessica was found dead on Creek Road behind the Pine Valley Condominium complex by Alex Wechter, age 10, at nine in

the morning on Tuesday, September 14. Early medical examiner reports indicate that she had been strangled. And as has been proven to be the case with the other victims, Jessica was also pregnant.

She is survived by her parents, Kimberly and Walter Frommel, who ask for any information in the capture of the person(s) responsible for taking the life of their only daughter. They are offering a ten thousand dollar reward...

"How the hell can Willie Zigs' prints be on anything? He's dead!" Agent Fielding from the Tactical Department exclaimed.

"You got me. We're dealing with some kind of genius here," Holloway replied.

"Come on. It doesn't make sense, and you know it, " Fielding said.

Holloway took a sip of water then continued, "Look, all I can deal with right now are the facts. We have the local authorities, the F.B.I., even Interpol involved."

"So you're just gonna wait around until he kills again?"

"No," Detective Holloway answered. "I'm gonna catch him."

Chapter 4

It was a late September Sunday morning and Garrison City woke up to its first frost. At six a.m, Trent Holloway sipped his coffee and pulled tautly on his tie. His boy was dressed in his little church outfit, a suit with solid blue pants and a plaid jacket. It should have been a day of rest for all but evil never sleeps.

Trent enjoyed watching the sunrise, the sparkling dew on the well-tended lawns stretched for many acres. The frost glistened like mystic glass, and tiny colorful prisms of light dotted the horizon. The birds were singing their bright songs and with each every passing moment, the day grew more beautiful. But underneath it all, like a gorgeous cover to an awful book, the environment was tainted. The Shallow Front Serial Killer, still at large, undermined the sweetness of the day.

The streets were mostly empty. People were either sleeping in or like Mr. and Mrs. Holloway, on their way to church. Church always made Trent feel better. It took him away to a place where, for a moment, he could forget all the evil in the world.

Sheila Holloway sat beside her husband. The soft orange glow of the early sun flattered her smooth honey-colored skin and made her even more beautiful. She didn't need but a touch of make-up which was always impeccably applied. Today, her lips were tinted a glistening shade of coral.

She was special, a women of finer things, but always concerned with the little things that truly mattered, the stuff that could easily be overlooked, that could be taken for granted. It was safe to say that Mrs. Holloway found the roses that others forgot to smell. Trent often felt deeply sorry that his wife wasn't able to have children of her own. But he was so glad that she was alive and still in his life.

After they were married, the newlyweds wanted to start a family right away. But a year later, not only was Sheila not pregnant but she had been experiencing wretched cramps and a lot of pain in her abdomen. She saw one of the ob/gyn physicians at the hospital. Within three days, she was diagnosed with ovarian cancer.

The doctors didn't give Sheila long to live. Trent was told that she had at most two months. He never told his wife.

They opted to undergo treatment with an experimental drug. In combination with chemotherapy and radiation, Sheila was very sick for many months. But she finally beat the cancer and had been in remission most of the years since.

"Do you think you'll catch him?" she asked almost in a whisper.

Lost in his thoughts, Trent didn't hear his wife's question.

"Honey, what do you think? Will you catch him?"

Sheila repeated.

"Yes, I do. I just don't know how yet. But I think he'll lose his stride, as animals sometimes do."

"I hope so. I worry about you so much. I never want to read about you in the paper," she said.

"You won't, until I arrest him," Trent assured her.

Sheila leaned over and kissed her husband's cheek just as he pulled into the driveway of the Shallow Front Lutheran Church.

"Daddy?" little Detton said from the back seat where he was playing with one of his action figures

"Yes, little man?"

"I love Jesus," he said.

"That's good, son," Holloway smiled at his son through the rearview mirror.

How could he have gotten Willie Zigs' fingerprints?

The Lutheran church was one of the oldest structures in Shallow Front. The next oldest was the cider mill in Lincoln which, much to the dismay of the older citizens, had been turned into a strip club called Vega. All hoped that the church would remain a church forever.

Pastor William Kline waited at the front doors as he did every Sunday morning, greeting the faithful with a warm handshake and a smile, his black robe swirling around him. Small square glasses rested on the bridge of his nose and bushy white eyebrows gave a certain distinction to his forehead.

"Welcome," he said to the Farmers who owned the Tulip Bell Bookstore downtown.

"Good morning," Pastor Kline said to the Waltons who owned a paving company in Harper.

"Wel..." Pastor Kline stopped short. His surprise gave way to joy as he realized the strong hand in his belonged to someone he hadn't seen in a while. Detective Trent Holloway.

"Well, well. It's good to see you here, Trent. I was wondering where you've been," he said with a smile.

Holloway laughed. "I'm sorry. I've been a very busy man lately. I should have known better than to skip out on you."

"Nonsense," Kline said. "What's important is that you are here now. And welcome, Mrs. Holloway."

"Hello, William," she replied.

The pastor saw little Detton smiling and holding a bible in his hand. "And how are you, little man?" the pastor asked.

"Hewo Pastor, sir," Detton said.

"Trent, one of these days we need to move that log out back, the one that fell last year. Someone is gonna trip over it," Kline said.

"Let's talk about it later. I'll take a look and see what I can do," Holloway said.

"Until later then," the pastor said before greeting the next in line.

The Holloway family took a seat by the organist. Sitting on a pew amongst the congregation of the church, Holloway felt better than he had in a long while. He needed spiritual cleansing, even if he was uncertain if he was a believer or not. As a homicide detective, he often questioned why God would let a serial killer walk the earth. For what purpose? Why would He let terror exist at all? Why have war, famine, poverty and disease?

Pastor Kline began his sermon with two songs to lift the hearts that were heavy with grief. Holloway could feel the sadness and desperation suspended like a dark cloud over all of them.

After the songs, Pastor Kline's commanding voice filled the church as he spoke to the congregation. "We all must repent. Sin is upon us. Let us take a moment to remember the victims of evil in our great city."

All bowed their heads in a moment of silence. A breeze from the east wafted through the church.

"And we thank God for his mercy."

Holloway was lost in thoughts of the serial killer the press had dubbed John Doe as Pastor Kline continued his homily. Where was he at that very moment? Was he sitting in church with them, hiding among the faithful, debasing the purity of the church with his evil?

"And I will give peace to the land, and ye shall lie down and none shall make you afraid, and I will rid evil beasts from of the land, neither shall the sword go through your land for I am the Lord God," Pastor Kline preached. "AMEN!"

The congregation responded in kind with a synchronized 'amen' that resounded throughout the church. Holloway sat quietly and listened.

Pastor Kline continued, "And ye shall chase your enemies, and they shall fall before you by the sword. But if you defy me on my covenant, I will bring a sword upon you and shall avenge the quarrel of my covenant, as you are gathered together in your cities. I will send pestilence upon you. You will be delivered into the hands of the enemy and of the beast."

Holloway sat straighter in his pew.

"People, we have a great many sins upon us. We of good faith cannot see the anger of God. But there is one among us who walks with much evil within him." Reading directly from the Good Book, Pastor Kline recited, "Blessed are the merciful, they will receive mercy. Blessed are the peacemakers for they will receive peace. They are the children of God. Take therefore no thought for the morrow, for the morrow shall take thought for the things of itself until the day the evil is thereof."

Pastor Kline asked everyone to rise and sing Glory, Glory Hallelujah.

After the service, Pastor Kline waited by the door once again, thanking people for coming. He looked back and saw Holloway at the end of the line.

When it was Mrs. Holloway's turn, he shook her hand, said his thanks, and then turned to Trent.

"Do you have a moment to speak now?" Kline asked.

"I just might. What would you like to tell me? You have something on your mind."

"Always the detective, I see," the pastor smiled.

"Can't help it," Holloway replied with a blush.

The morning had turned dreary. Pastor Kline guided Trent back into the shelter of the church. As he watched the young detective, he saw a tall man with a youthful face and premature gray hair sprouting at his temples. The trench coat he wore didn't cover up the fact that Trent had lost weight.

"I was hoping," Kline began, "you could help mend my heart a bit."

Trent was surprised. "How can I help?"

Kline grimaced, took off his glasses and wiped the left lens before placing them back on the bridge of his nose.

"Do you have any leads on the killer's identity? Please tell me you do."

"No, I'm afraid not. The newspapers have pretty much reported all we have. Lots of clues, none make sense," Holloway answered cautiously.

"Yes, I know. I've been reading the newspaper and watching Channel 6. This evil man prays on women, pregnant women. Do you believe this is coincidence?" the pastor asked sincerely.

"I don't," Holloway said. "But it doesn't matter what I believe. What matters is that we catch this maniac."

"Oh, I disagree Trent, my son. It does matter what you believe. It always matters."

Holloway glanced at the idol of Jesus on the altar, then back at Kline. "You're right. Sometimes, though, I'm afraid of what I will find," Holloway said.

Pastor William Kline placed a hand on the detective's shoulder and looked at Jesus' likeness as Holloway looked the other way.

"Behold I send you forth as a sheep in the midst of wolves."

Holloway looked at Pastor Kline and smiled sadly.

"Good luck to you, my friend," Pastor Kline said.

Holloway walked from the church into the rain, pulled his coat over his head and ran to the car.

Across town, Detective Frank Lion spent the evening with his wife and two sons. They played a board game and laughed. Frank's laughter, however, was forced and strangled with something else. It took him only a few seconds to realize it was guilt.

He knew that if he confessed his affair with the waitress from Gussby's, he would lose her forever. And if his wife found out about the two of them on her own, he would lose even more than that.

Darla Goodman sat at the card table in her kitchen and drank a glass of wine with a half a bologna sandwich. Sitting on the old carpet, his feet tucked under his legs, her son Michael played video games. She listened as he enthusiastically shot down airplanes.

What am I doing anyway?

As she lit a cigarette, she gave what was left of her half a sandwich to the dog and asked her son, "Mikey, do you want the other half of this sandwich?"

"No mommy. No thanks," he politely answered.

"Not too much longer, okay?" she let out a stream of bluish white smoke. "Tomorrow you have school, okay?"

Mikey looked up at her, blonde curls cascading across his forehead.

"Kay mommy."

What am I gonna do? she thought. A cool breeze drifted in through a crack in the door and hugged her body. Shivering, she looked out at the park where the older kids were playing basketball.

Sure is getting cooler. Winter will be here in no time. Darla poured herself another glass of scarlet wine and thought about her situation. Her last man, the one whom she was sure she'd marry, left after he learned she was pregnant with Mikey and never came back. And here she was again, in love, no, in something even deeper than love, and pregnant again. *What is love anyway?* she asked herself. *And why can't I ever seem to catch a break?*

Although she didn't want them to, her thoughts drifted to her past. Her youth until the age of twelve was vivid, and she could remember everything. After that, it all became a spiraling black blur.

She had met her first boyfriend, Jeffrey Houston, at a soda shop. It had all started with a simple hello. She was fifteen. They looked into each other's eyes with great sympathy and clicked right away.

She had kissed him that same night, one small peck that sealed a promise to go out together the next weekend. Jeffrey went home and was beaten by his father for being five minutes late. But Jeff had it easy, much easier than she ever did.

Darla's father did other things to her. Not because she was late. Just because. And it continued for many more nights, always without reason. Or, more appropriately, always for any reason.

She was punished for being a 'bad girl'. She was punished worse for being a 'good girl'.

Her father was a drunk. He worked for Garrison City Water Works as a plumber. He beat his wife every chance he got. He threw her down the stairs once and broke both her legs. But he would never hurt his daughter like that. No, he would never do that. He found other things to do instead.

He was a man who got excited by little girls. And his little girl was special. Especially when she brought home a report card filled with A's. To him, that was fucking the best. When she was naughty though...

But that's not true either and you know it.

Darla had a sneaking suspicion that her father's abuse had been going on for a long time but she couldn't remember. *Why can't I remember?*

She stared long and hard at her glass of wine. She needed to remember. So she closed her eyes and drifted off in thought. *Remember!*

Then she did. She was twelve when her father first sexually molested her, although at the time, she didn't know what he was doing to her. All she knew was that it hurt.

Sometimes a whole month would go by and her body would heal but then he'd touch her again and rip her apart all over again. She would go down, in a blur of time, like a little girl drowning in quicksand.

When had it become an addiction, though? How many men have I fucked? A hundred? One twenty?

Jeffrey french kissed her on their first real date that following weekend and took her to lunch at Whistle Jack's. They spent the day and early evening together, trading stories of their hopes and dreams. From the night sky, they picked a brightly shining star and claimed it as their very own. They named it and fantasized that they owned it. Jeffrey told her that he would risk being beaten again for just one more minute with her.

When he returned home ten minutes late, Jeffrey's father was waiting for him at the top of the stairs with his belt. Jeffrey slowly climbed the stairs to where his father waited, expecting to be punished as usual in the study at the top of the stairs. Instead, his father pushed him down the stairs. Jeffrey died of a broken neck because he wanted one more minute with Darla.

That I remember, she thought.

Darla was crushed. And had been every day since. When her father decided to molest her just before Jeffrey's funeral, she died inside. When her mother died of cancer two years later, her father repeated the scene. Darla left home then and stayed with a boy in Bennington. At eighteen, she graduated from high school and left the state to join the navy.

She enlisted for a four-year term and received a government scholarship for college. The navy years were good years.

Darla learned that her father had died from heart problems. The police said that they found him dead in his easy chair. In his left hand, he held Darla's photo. His face was blue and puffy from the heart attack.

Darla enrolled in college at twenty-three. She chose business management as her major and met Nicholas Jarnis, a bright, handsome boy, in her political science class. Nicholas was a science major, animal behavior. He was so charming and good-looking, Darla fell hard for him.

Two months after they had met, Darla found out that she was pregnant with Nicholas' baby. With her future ruined, Darla dropped out of college. With his future ruined, Nick left town and never returned.

Darla tried to get child support from him, and for five

years, the struggle to pull herself out of the quicksand had become horrifyingly familiar. With her little child always first in her mind, Darla suffered through several dead-end jobs. She eventually wound up in Shallow Front with yet another dead-end job, but at least she had a home in the old trailer and a dog Mikey could play with.

Luckily, Darla still had her looks. And wanting desperately to change her son's life, she decided to use them to her advantage. She decided to charge money for sex. Her intention had always been to use the money to better her son's future. She was going to get them out of the trailer park and into a real home.

She had been with so many nameless men, she lost track. Sometimes she would learn their names during the meager conversations before sex, but in the end, it was all the same.

She began to cry at the kitchen table. She never felt more sorry for herself than she did then. She was a disgrace, and her heart ached every time she thought about Mikey finding out what she did to make money. Then she thought about Frank and realized that she was crying because of her feelings for him.

"Time for bed," she said. He turned off his video game and stood up. *What a good boy I have,* she thought.

"Get your jammies on now," she said as she followed her son back to his bedroom.

"Are we gonna have sweet dreams tonight?"

"Yes, mommy."

"And no boogie men, right?"

"No boogie men, mommy."

Darla kissed her son and tucked him into his own little bed. He had created a special world for himself with cartoon characters and drawings taped to the walls of his room. A model rocket hung from the ceiling on a string, and he had pasted the glow-in-the-dark stars she had bought him all around it. He had even named one of the stars.

After she was sure that Mikey was asleep, she returned to the kitchen table, poured herself another glass of wine and cried again without worrying that he might hear her.

Detective Frank Lion had visited Darla many times. He was her sweetest customer, always leaving a hundred dollars instead of the fifty she asked for and bringing good bottles of wine for her to enjoy after he left. Darla sipped wine from one of them now.

Frank talked to her. He spoke of his work, of his wife and of his secret desires, desires he could never share with the woman he married. Lately, he talked a lot about the serial killer on the loose in Shallow Front. Frank used the word 'slaughtering' instead of killing and it scared her. And he talked about Billy Warrington.

Darla came to terms with her feelings about Frank's wife, Deb, because of the way Frank talked about her. The woman did not make Frank happy. In fact, she had made his life hell with her constant complaining and nagging.

Frank liked Darla because Darla always understood. He once told her that she was a dove dodging the lightning above the darkest clouds.

Frank was very sweet and had always been her favorite. It didn't matter to Darla that he was a bit overweight. She looked past it and saw him for who he was. And that was why Darla let Frank have her without a condom.

"I prefer the good stuff," Frank always said.

Darla knew that he preferred sex without a condom and because he was married, she thought it would be OK. "Frank, we have to be careful."

"Honey, you don't wear gloves to hold an angel's hand," he told her.

Four weeks ago, just before her period, she and Frank had unprotected sex. And there she was, pregnant and in the quicksand again.

Darla didn't know how she would tell Frank. But in truth, she was much more worried about the stalker of pregnant women. Somehow he would find out that she was pregnant. She was terrified.

How was Darla going to hide her pregnancy from a man with no identity? He was an evil so terrible that for the first time in the town's history, people were locking doors and windows at night before they went to sleep. Holdeman's Hardware had run out of chain locks.

The killer was a man but not a man at all.

Darla imagined him again as she saw him that horrible night, standing on the other side of the street, wearing a low brimmed hat as dark as night itself. He wore a trench coat equally as black. She remembered his eyes, shining, red and terrifying. Yet they were somehow...

Sexy?

She was afraid and confused all over again.

Darla knew from Frank that the killer left behind fingerprints of dead people. And somehow, he escaped each crime scene unnoticed.

How could a woman not get lost in those eyes? They were smoldering with passion and desire. A woman would look into those eyes and freeze in place like she was stuck in dried cement.

Darla imagined the smell of his cologne and the magnetic something else she couldn't identify. And in his masculine, brute voice he claimed to be the taker of takers, the ultimate evil, as sharp as his own will.

Just like her father. Just like Mikey's father.

He was no different than any other man. Hidden under the brim of his hat, Darla was sure that he was nobody special.

Frank Lion was.

Were his eyes really like I saw them across from Gussby's? Did they really glow?

Chapter 5

On the east side of Garrison was a small community park. As the weather turned cold, fewer and fewer children played there, preferring instead to stay inside in front of the television with their video games and sitcoms. The slides and swings were empty, and the summer air that was once filled with joyful screams was eerily silent.

On October 15th, the city imposed an indefinite curfew. Those leaving their homes after seven in the evening were to be stopped and questioned, and they had better have a good reason for being out late.

The investigation into the murders of Cassandra Evans, Amanda Dawson and Jessica Frommel remained unresolved, and as horrible as it was to admit, the police had no choice but to wait for another attack. Sadly something else needed to happen in order to either capture the killer or gather more clues.

Jeremy Harris drove to the community park in his Jeep that afternoon and sat by the small pond to watch the ducks. He glanced at the huge wooden cross donated by the Spring Garden Hospital for the children to climb and hang on. School was still in session and a crisp breeze chilled the air. He doubted he would see any children running around and playing but he prayed silently anyway for their safety.

Do you see what eye see?

Still rattled by the events at the station house, he sat quietly, lost in thought. He pulled out a pack of menthol cigarettes and lit one with his disposable lighter. A bluish flame flared.

Do you see what eye see?

Harris could not eradicate the image of that horrible statue of the angel from his memory. It dominated his dreams and turned them into nightmares. Captain Pullman had been right to give him a few days off. That first night, he slept restlessly. The driving rain kept him company but could not obliterate the ominous feelings he had in his heart. He woke up reaching for his gun.

Harris remembered his dream from that night. He walked towards an old house suffering badly from weather and age. He heard someone shaking an empty spray can as he approached it. The sound was similar to a rattlesnake's vibrating tail.

Jeremy walked along gravel that felt ancient. The small stones crumbled beneath his feet and kicked up little plumes of dust. He looked ahead and noticed that the house had a steep, sloping roof on both sides.

The shingles on the roof peeled up like dead bark. The windows, although boarded up, looked like gaping eye sockets. He felt as if the house itself was watching him come closer and closer.

The front door opened on ancient hinges and screamed in protest. Rust flaked off of them in large crispy chunks.

The warped door creaked open and revealed an empty hallway with stairs and broken tooth-like rails.

As he entered the house, a musty odor assaulted his senses. The smell was so real and so pungent. It was the smell of dried blood, a thousand years old yet as fresh as yesterday. The odor of death soaked into his nostrils.

The first room he entered had hardwood flooring that he knew was once slick with heavily polished varnish. But in his dream it was rotten, floorboards irregularly jutted up at odd angles and most were warped from dampness and neglect. Jeremy turned towards the staircase. The door at the top of the stairs was halfway open. A blinding light trickled down and illuminated the landing and dark hallway.

Jeremy could barely see the paintings on the walls. But with each step up the stairs, they became clearer. But he could never really make out their subjects and could never really see them no matter how hard he tried.

Who will paint for me?

As he approached the door, he saw that a rusty number '6' was nailed onto it. It was forged of iron and looked very old. The number taunted him. Why was it there? Jeremy pushed the door all the way open and tripped and fell onto a concrete floor covered with thousands of drains.

From a dark corner of the room, a low growl pricked his ears. And from the shadows, an ominous mouth lined with razor sharp teeth revealed itself. Jeremy watched as the face of a gray wolf inched from the dark. A long body slowly followed as the beast lumbered toward him in slow motion.

Around its neck was a gold badge.

Jeremy was badly frightened. His heart beat wildly. He ran backwards, trying to find a safe exit from certain death.

He fell backwards against the wall as the killer wolf descended on him. It dragged a length of chain behind it. Jeremy heard the heavy links scrape against the coarse floor. He felt an intense heat flare from the nostrils of the wolf as it charged at him in a hellish rage.

Jeremy felt a ripping pain in torso. He was pinned against a wall. When he looked down, he saw a jagged antler protruding from his chest. His lungs filled with blood and his eyes rolled wildly in their sockets as his jaw dropped. In one horrible moment, he realized that he would drown in his own blood. But the nightmare was far from over.

The wolf wailed maniacally and whipped its head from side to side trying to grab the gold badge attached to its chain. It infuriated the creature that he couldn't reach it, and it growled in utter rage.

With no other outlet for its anger, the gray wolf lunged at the detective who was helplessly pinned against the wall like a poster. As he was dying under the bright light, Jeremy Harris saw the beast's horrid gleaming eyes, the color of streetlights and caution, filled with absolute rage, devoid of pity. The gaping mouth stabbed like a knife at the detective's lower abdomen and ripped it open. Harris watched in horror as his intestines unraveled and fell to the floor. Then, as he maneuvered his head in a last ditch effort to spot something that would lead him to freedom, he saw the white porcelain angel. It was in a different corner of the room and in the same pose of prayer as when he had first seen it on his desk that fateful day, looking up at heaven. Jeremy looked up in the same direction before realizing that the angel's eyes sockets were leaking red blood. His last shocked gaze revealed that the eyes no longer belonged to Jessica Frommel. They belonged to him.

Jeremy woke up each night then.

The dreams had all been identical to the first, except for the last one, last night. In it, he saw a man in a black trench coat and a broad brimmed hat. He smiled as the gray wolf tore into Jeremy's abdomen. He held the chain like a leash and had given it enough slack so that the wolf could reach its prey.

"Do you see what eye see?" the man asked.

In the dream, Jeremy tried to answer, but his mouth was filled with blood.

"Stay out of this, Detective, and I won't let go of the leash," the man with the hat whispered.

This morning, after the latest version of the dream, Detective Harris woke up screaming.

Jeremy lit another menthol cigarette and walked to his car. As he drove away from Carson Park, the irony of the cross in the playground struck him particularly hard.

Darla Goodman wrapped herself in a blanket because she could not afford to pay the heating bill that month. Little Mikey was sleeping at a friend's house for a few nights until she earned enough money to pay the bill.

At eleven fifteen in the morning, Darla heard a friendly knock at her door. She looked out the peephole and saw a smiling Frank Lion.

She smiled as she opened the door. Frank was dressed in his work clothes and held a bag of groceries in his arms.

"I don't have an appointment," Frank said.

"That's okay," she whispered as she relieved him of the brown grocery bag.

"Son home?"

Darla smiled and brushed her black bangs from her eyes. "No. He's at a friend's. I'm glad you're here, Frank. I need a favor," Darla said shyly.

"Of me?" he asked. "What could I possibly do for you?"

Darla looked down at the floor, obviously embarrassed to have to ask Frank for help. A single tear ran down her pale cheek. "I have no heat."

Frank Lion stepped forward and hugged her.

"Now you do, baby..." he cooed. "Now you do."

Frank kissed Darla gently on the forehead and cupped her face in his hand. As he looked deep into her eyes, he kissed her again with an intensity that surprised him. He slid the blanket off her shoulders and carried it to the bed. She met him there and watched as he pulled off his pants then her bathrobe.

I'm not in the quicksand with Frank, Darla thought as he entered her. She wrapped her legs around him. She loved every move he made and under his body, blossomed in a way she never knew she could.

Darla had never known romance until Frank. During their lovemaking, he transported her to beautiful places where nothing else mattered. Today he lasted longer than usual. Her body was no longer in the cold trailer but in a wild place of ferns and waterfalls. They were making love on a flat rock warmed by the sun, naked to the sky. Suddenly, the rain fell in torrents. As the drops hit their hot bodies, steam shrouded them in a warm, romantic cloud.

Darla moaned and rocked harder against Frank. He sensed that she was close and waited to explode just as she began to.

They made love until they couldn't anymore.

Detective Lion rested beside Darla in bliss just as Detective Jeremy Harris drove his Jeep for the very last time.

"I can't stay long. I finish work at three," he said as he slipped her a bundle of money. "Here's two hundred. You'll have heat now."

"Oh, Frank. You have no idea how much I lov... um, I mean owe you."

"Nonsense, Darla," Frank said.

Frank prepared a lavish lunch. They ate without their clothes on as the sun warmed the trailer.

After the meal, Frank sat back against the chair.

"I can hardly breathe," Darla said, holding a hand over her stomach.

"You! I'm so full I couldn't breathe if you held a gun to my head."

Darla laughed.

"So how are things?" he asked with concern.

"Well, I don't work nights anymore at Gussby's."

"Why not?" Frank asked.

Darla hesitated and licked her lower lip. "I lost my

job." The tears came all at once. "I lost my...my..."

Darla began sobbing so hard, she crumpled to the floor. Frank caught her in his arms and pulled her close to his chest.

"It's okay, baby. It's okay. I'll take care of you. I will always take care of you," he said as he rocked her in his arms like a child.

Darla knew Frank meant what he said and started crying even harder. She had to tell him right now. "Wh...wha...what am I go-gonna d-do, Frank? I-I'm pre-pregnant," she breathed into his neck, fearful of his reaction.

He loosened his grip and stared at her in shock. "It's okay, Darla," he said after a brief pause. He closed his eyes and held her tight, wondering if the baby was his. After all, you don't wear gloves when you hold an angel's hand.

"We'll get through this together," he said as he tilted her wet face up to his. "We will. I promise."

Detective Lion reached into his pocket and pulled out a gold cross on a gold chain. A red ruby adorned its center.

"I want you to have this," he whispered, his lips close to hers. "I want you to have this because I know you believe in me."

"Yes I do," she whispered back.

"And if you believe and I believe..." he started, "...what do we have to worry about?"

Frank picked her up, carried her to the back bedroom and made love to her one more time.

Jeremy Harris drove his Jeep down Carson Boulevard, a mile from the Shallow Front city limit. One of the benefits of being a cop was that you didn't have to obey the speed limit signs and could drive as you wished. But something he saw out of the corner of his eye stopped him from speeding. *No, it can't be,* he thought.

At the intersection of Second and Third Streets, a line of people waited for the county bus at the bus stop. And among them was the man from his dreams.

The man who held the leash.

He was dressed in a black pinstriped suit with a deep red tie. The black brimmed hat was tilted just as Jeremy remembered. The demonic yellow eyes were not visible, however. Jeremy knew the man couldn't be real. How could he be, unless he was back home in bed, fast asleep, dreaming? And Jeremy was quite certain that he wasn't.

Who will paint for me?

He put the Jeep in third gear and gunned it away from the intersection as fast as he could. Rolling hills and woods replaced the buildings and stores which became fewer and farther between. Detective Harris never looked back.

He wasn't real, you asshole, he said to himself. *But keep moving anyway because you know who holds the leash.*

Suddenly, Jeremy had a wild desire run the man down, to drive back to the intersection and to aim the Jeep at him.

Harris was as surprised to find himself in fifth gear as he was to find himself afraid of an imaginary creature. But then, he wasn't sure that the man wasn't real. *Who could he be?* he thought. *But it doesn't matter because one thing is for certain. He holds the leash and that's reason enough to fear him.*

Do you see what eye see?

Jeremy spun his head around. The voice was in his Jeep. He turned to look behind him. On the back seat were two bloody eyeballs rolling from left to right.

One green, one blue.

He faced the road again, panicked by what was in his car, but knowing that he had to remain focused on the road. It was too late. He swerved out of his lane. A cement truck was bearing down on him. There was no time to maneuver. The truck crashed into the detective's Jeep with so much force that the driver's head slammed against the windshield and fractured it into a spiderweb of glass. Harris' Jeep flipped several times and came to rest in a twisted mass of metal. Shattered glass rained down over the Jeep as the truck plowed on through. Jeremy ducked as the ragtop roof caved in over his head. His face slammed into the dashboard, the impact shattering his front teeth and breaking his nose. He bit his tongue in half and felt the stick shift rip through his back into his lungs. Jeremy Harris' last thought was *This is my last ride.*

At two-thirty that afternoon, the State Police and Spring Garden authorities arrived at the scene of the accident. There had been no witnesses so no one was able to tell how it all had happened. The cement truck laid like a carcass on the shoulder of the road. The driver was dead, partially decapitated by a shard of glass from the windshield.

The Jeep had come to a stop upside down, its

destroyed front end in the back seat. The only things alive and moving were the windshield wipers which smeared blood instead of water. Jeremy Harris' body was twisted up into the engine. His legs were fifteen feet away in a ditch. Both hips had been shattered. Upon seeing the knobs of grayish bone and cartilage, the traffic cop first at the scene vomited.

Jeremy Harris was pronounced dead at two forty-five. Trent Holloway and Captain Pullman arrived at three.

"Oh my dear Christ," Pullman said. The only part of Jeremy still relatively intact was his face. A fly had parked itself on his bloody lower lip.

"He had no family," Pullman said.

"Yes he did, sir," Holloway said. "He had us."

A solemn moment of silence passed between the two policemen as they looked at the wreckage.

"What do you suppose happened, Captain?" Holloway asked.

"I'm not sure, Trent."

Why couldn't Jeremy catch that pass? Trent's father said in his mind.

The afternoon was cooling down by the time the police finished with the accident scene.

"All I can say is that this place, our city, seems to have gone bad," Holloway observed. "Sir, I don't think this was a DUI ."

"I believe you're right about that," Pullman said. "I-I can't believe Harris is dead. I just called to check on him yesterday."

Holloway looked up at the tops of nearby trees. The odor of spilled gasoline and oil mingled with the coppery tang of blood. *If only the trees could talk.*

"It comes quick," Pullman said, staring at the void of the woods.

"What does?" Trent asked.

"The end. It sneaks up on you when you least expect it."

Holloway looked over at the Captain and an eerie feeling of resentment overwhelmed him.

"Jesus, I can't fucking believe..." Pullman started but couldn't finish. He put his hand up to his mouth and tried to hold in his sobs. Seeing Pullman that way made Holloway's soul drown in sorrow.

To change the mood, Holloway reverted to being a cop. "It looks like he was going very fast judging from the tire marks on the road. It also appears as though he was speeding from something," Holloway added.

"The impact of the collision was insane," Pullman grimaced.

"His body is twisted underneath the goddamn motor, his neck is brok..."

Another sudden burst of tears, but this time from Holloway.

He cleared his eyes and looked into the death trap that was once his colleague's Jeep. Detective Holloway saw his broken friend laying in the middle of hell, an innocent man eaten alive by some perverse demon. But it was Jeremy's face that he would never forget. His gaping mouth had been frozen in a silent scream, as if Jeremy stared into the face of a nightmare as he died.

Chapter 6

In the depths of his broken heart, a shallow pool of blood runs hot. In this pool, the demons of hell wait to be released into his bloodstream. At the slightest sinister thought, they empty into his veins and rejoice at their escape from the deep and lonely place. To their own straightjacket rhythms, they dance like madmen as they invade the purer thoughts that live inside him and reveal themselves from the shadows.

It has been over three weeks since he has made a woman scream, since he has watched a life empty into his hands and felt the heat of beauty turn to the icy death he so longs for.

But we cannot forget the cop.

No, we can't.

He no longer owns the dark corners of the policeman's mind so he must hide in the open. Today, he sits on the roof of the Shallow Front Bank like a dark crow, thinking how it is now time to really get down to business.

Willie Zigs couldn't work for me. Neither could Bill Warrington.

All Hallow's Eve is Friday, the day before the Shallow Front Fair and the day that Detective Jeremy Harris will be buried.

What a fine day that would be to get down to business.

Sheila Holloway tried to pull herself together in the bathroom. Her husband busied himself in the bedroom, adjusting his white funeral gloves. The death of Jeremy Harris hurt Holloway in many different places. Others would fail to understand if he tried to explain. But his wife did. Sheila understood that the place beneath the badge was where the soul resided.

In the dress uniform that he has had no occasion to wear in the last five years, Holloway thought back to when River Detton died. River had been a tough cop, perhaps one of the best Spring Garden ever had, and Trent's friend. His style was to shoot first and ask questions later. Luckily, his instincts were always on target.

Trent thought about River now because he, like Jeremy Harris, died alone — unmarried and without children. There were other similarities between the two men but in reality, they were very different.

Holloway's thoughts brought him back to that fateful day when Spring Garden and Shallow Front were innocent. River had just made Sergeant. It was near Christmas.

On a very cold winter's day, Trent received a phone call from Captain Pullman who was on special assignment. He was stationed at Shallow Front Community Hospital.

A two-day-old infant lay in an incubator fighting for its life. It had been born six weeks premature. The parents of the child were true unfortunates. They had no home and slept in cardboard boxes, eating what others threw away. They had copulated under the moon in the Garrison City park.

The infant's mother's name was Helen, but as Holloway straightened his tie, he couldn't for the life of him remember the father's.

Just shy of eight months later, the baby was born prematurely. Social Services stepped in immediately.

Sheila Holloway was the nurse who attended the infant. It was her responsibility to call Social Services if a case required it. And as much as she didn't want to take him away from his mother, she knew she had to find the baby a home with four plaster, not cardboard, walls.

Of course Helen wanted the best for her child, but she had lost her job a year and a half prior and was without means to support him. Her husband had lost everything he owned to the IRS. They tried to get help but had been turned away from every door they knocked on. They had no choice but to live on the dirty streets.

The second day the baby was in the incubator, the street people came to see their child and were stopped by an agent from Child Welfare. They were not allowed to go near the baby until their case had been reviewed. Helen was torn apart by grief and her husband was angry. He had threatened to return and take his baby out of the hospital. River Detton was assigned guard duty.

River guarded not only the nurse's station but the incubators as well. He stood beside the door like a soldier, his arms behind his back, new sergeant's stripes freshly sewn on his sleeve.

His orders were to prohibit anyone from getting near the baby who was not a doctor or a nurse. Sergeant Detton himself was not permitted inside the room unless specifically requested by hospital personnel.

"Guard the child with your life," Captain Pullman had ordered.

And he did.

Helen, the homeless, grief stricken mother, showed up early two mornings later and pulled a nine millimeter from her ripped jacket. She fired three times at Detton. Two rounds were stopped by his bulletproof vest. One entered his brain and killed him.

When Sheila returned with fresh sheets for the infants a moment later, she saw the insanity in the mother's eyes as she struggled to unhook the IVs attached to her tiny son. Tears ran down her dirty cheeks and made lanes of cleanliness on her haggard face. Helen grabbed her baby and ran to the hospital parking lot.

Officer David Squall had been getting coffee for River when he heard the shots. He dropped the coffee and ran towards the woman who was holding a baby in one hand and firing a gun with the other.

Squall shot and killed the woman and saved the baby's life. After the baby matured in the incubator, Social Services intervened and took care of him. Sheila and Trent Holloway adopted him shortly thereafter. Trent named his son Detton after the officer who had given his life to protect him.

Sheila struggled with the images imprinted on her memory of the officer being shot in the head. She went for psychotherapy for an entire year after the incident.

So did Officer David Squall. His enormous guilt over killing the child's mother tore at his confidence and made him a danger to himself and to others on the job.

Trent did not have to struggle with those memories and remembered his friend as full of life and laughter. In fact, he remembered him every time he looked at his son.

River Detton's wake and funeral service included a closed casket. Sheila wept pitifully the entire service. She felt responsible for the officer's death.

The homeless father whose name Holloway couldn't remember was William Nolan. He jumped from the Susquehanna River Bridge in Pennsylvania two days after he learned of his wife's death.

So many years ago.

Detton Holloway walked into the bedroom wearing his Sunday suit and carrying his bible.

"You wook nice, daddy."

"Why thank you, champ. So do you. How about after this, we get some ice cream?" Trent asked his son.

Detton was delighted. "Ice cweam! Ice cweam! Yay!" He jumped from his father's arms and ran to tell his mother.

At the kitchen table, Sheila drank her coffee and watched the drizzle outside. Trent approached her with a serious look on his face.

"You okay?" he asked.

"I'm fine. I've just been thinking," his wife replied.

"Thinking about what, honey?"

Sheila looked down at her hands. "I'm afraid for us all, Trent. I pray to God every day to keep you safe and for you to catch this awful man. I worry about you."

"I will catch him, honey. You know I will," Trent said to calm her.

"I can't believe Jeremy is dead," Sheila cried. Tears ran down her face and into her coffee. "I didn't know him well, but he was a cop just like you. And when I think of him," she wiped her eyes, "I think of you."

Holloway felt goose bumps crawl down his left arm. But they quickly disappeared as Detton ran into the kitchen and jumped in his arms.

"Nothing is gonna happen," Holloway said.

"You promise?" she asked as she dabbed at her wet nose.

"Cross my heart..." Holloway stopped before finishing the rest of the old saying.

And hope to die.

The Holloways arrived at Miller's Funeral Home shortly after eight-thirty that morning. Officer David Squall greeted them at the door.

"Good morning, Detective," Squall said.

"Good morning Officer. We sure meet in a bad place this morning, don't we?"

"Yes, sir. Unfortunately we sure do," replied Squall.

"Trent!" a voice called from behind. Captain Pullman was with his wife.

Holloway turned. "Hello sir."

"Morning. Listen, has Heather arrived yet?"

"Heather? Oh, you mean Mills. Well I just got here myself and don't really know who's here or not," Holloway said.

"Well, the reason I'm asking is because she and Jeremy were good friends. She was his secretary but..." Pullman didn't finish his sentence.

"Captain what's wrong?"

"Since he hadn't any family, no wife, no kids, the beneficiaries of his life insurance policy were the Lutheran Church and the police force. I want to give Heather the police force's share." The sorrow in Captain Pullman's voice tugged at Holloway's strained composure.

"Sounds nice, Captain. I'm sure she'd accept it," Holloway said. "Now if you'll excuse me, sir." Trent turned from Pullman.

Pastor Kline caught Holloway's attention.

"Good morning, William," Holloway said as he caught up to the clergyman. The look on Kline's face was unsettling. He appeared to be under the influence of some drug. His eyes were vacant and empty.

"Are you alright?" Holloway asked.

Kline barely turned his head.

"Pastor Kline?"

"Oh, Trent, my son. How are you?"

Trent realized that the pastor wore an expression of sleeplessness and fear. "William, what's wrong with you?"

"Just tired is all," Kline wearily replied. He suddenly lurched forward and leaned heavily on a table. "I haven't slept for almost a week."

Holloway's interest was piqued. "Why not?" he asked.

"Well, it sounds ridiculous, but I have been having very bad dreams. Horrible images all night long," the Pastor replied.

"What kind of dreams?" Trent was curious. "You mean

nightmares?"

"I mean the most horrifying dreams you could imagine." Kline closed his eyes. "I guess they are nightmares. About Shallow Front. And there's always this door..." Kline seemed too exhausted to continue, but he straightened up and smoothed out his black robe. "I've been having a recurring dream about an old house. And every time I walk up to it, I see a door with a number six on it."

Holloway spoke softly, "Do you ever open the door?"

William's eyes came to life as if Trent had just read his mind. "Yes, I do. And when I do there's..."

"Holloway," Frank Lion interrupted. Trent jumped at Frank's hand on his shoulder.

"Frank. How've you been?"

"It's been rough. I can't believe one of us is gone," Frank responded with his usual bravado.

Pastor Kline sensed it was time to leave the two cops alone. "If you would excuse me, gentlemen," he nodded and slipped through the back door of the viewing room.

"Deb and I don't even know how to behave," Lion said.

"I know. It's hit me pretty hard, too."

"Killed off duty he was, Trent," Lion said, his eyes wide with conviction. "Between you and me, I can't swallow all the shit Pullman's been feeding the force about Jeremy's wreck."

"What do you mean? I haven't heard anything," Trent said, genuinely surprised.

Detective Lion leaned in closer to Holloway's ear. "Jeremy had an exceptionally clean driving record. In fact, better than anyone else's on the force. And," he added, "his Jeep hadn't been tampered with in any way."

"I know, Frank, it's fucked up. But what are you getting at?"

"Notice that we haven't heard a peep out of killer in three weeks?" Frank posed the question suggestively.

"Oh, he's still around. I can feel it," Trent said. "Frank, are you thinking that Jeremy was killed by our guy?"

"Yeh, that's what I'm thinking," Frank Lion replied.

"Trent, how the hell do we sleep at night?" Lion asked.

"Scotch," Holloway said. "I need a cigarette. Care to join me?"

"No, thanks. I don't want to leave Deb alone. She might lose it again." Detective Lion smiled sadly as Holloway walked out into the dreary afternoon. It had been raining on and off all day.

Trent stood under the awning at the back of Miller's and lit a cigarette. *What if the killer did somehow get to Jeremy? What can I do about it?* He realized that there was nothing he could do. He was a man with his hands tied in frustration and despair. *I'm never gonna solve this.*

Yet it wasn't over. And Trent knew he had to do something about it. He meant what he said to his captain. Something had gone bad in their city, and he couldn't put his finger on it. Something very wrong,

The back door of the funeral home opened and from its shadows, Pastor William Kline emerged. "I thought I'd find you out here. I've got five minutes before the service begins. Then we both need to go back in."

"Go on then," Trent urged. "I want you to tell me about the dreams."

Kline began.

"When I approach the door with the number six dead in the center, I hear a sound. I don't know how to describe it exactly. Maybe it's whistling through cotton or maybe a marble being shaken in a can. Anyway, when I open the door, the sound gets louder, and then I see it."

"See what?" Trent asked.

"Antlers." Kline seemed almost embarrassed saying the word.

"Deer antlers?"

"Yes. Massive deer antlers. Dozens of ten-point racks everywhere. Then I see paintings. I can never quite make them out, or maybe I can and just can't remember."

"I don't know what to think, William. Maybe you're crazy," Trent joked to lighten the mood.

"Thanks a lot, Detective," Pastor Kline said with his first genuine smile of the day. "Isn't it true that dreams really mean something?"

"That's what the shrinks always say," Trent agreed.

"Well, at least in my dreams, I get a back door, a way out. But every time I try to get to it, these great gray wolves come out of nowhere and block my exit. I tell you, Trent. I have never seen wolves like these."

Teeth like an Alaskan wolf would have.

Holloway felt a chill crawl up his neck not caused by the damp air.

Kline continued, "Anyway, I always wake up when I'm trapped by the wolves. And the strangest thing is that I smell burning matches. Like someone just lit a pack of them and blew them out in my bedroom."

Holloway froze. "I don't know what it all means, Pastor. But I don't think you're in any danger," Holloway said as a strip of light broke through the clouds.

Dreams always mean something.

"Thank you for listening, Detective. I'll see you inside."

The service lasted thirty minutes. Trent was thankful that the casket was closed. It was bad enough that he would forever have the image of Jeremy in his memory, twisted to pieces inside a mangled Jeep, a fly on his lip.

The ride to the graveyard for the conclusion of the funeral service made Trent nervous.

Sheila checked on Detton in the back seat before speaking to her husband. Her son was busy playing with his toy trucks.

"I think we should have left him with a sitter, Trent," Sheila said.

"Why? Life isn't always about being happy. There's this part, too. He'll be fine," Trent replied with a touch of annoyance.

"He's a bit young..." Sheila began to protest.

Trent interrupted, "Don't worry. He's a smart little boy. He'll understand."

The Holloways followed the hearse and three patrol cars. Behind them, every off duty cop in the county completed the procession.

Pastor Kline delivered his funeral sermon with the twenty one gun salute. Holloway listened intently.

"And though I walk through the valley of the shadow of death..." and on the pastor spoke.

Afterwards, Holloway had the honor of folding the American flag. He had done the same for River Detton.

How many other flags will I fold? he wondered.

Flanked on each side by five policemen, Heather Mills stood unsteadily. Trent said a silent prayer when he had finished folding the flag and lifted it from the coffin. He stepped in front of Heather and placed it in her hands. She cried uncontrollably along with the other mourners. It was a very sad day in Shallow Front.

Trent saluted crisply, hiding his own sorrow, and stepped back.

When he lowered his hand, he saw a great oak tree in the distance. It was very old with vast limbs. To his surprise, a man was leaning against the trunk. He wore a black suit, the type one would wear to a funeral, and a hat that obscured his features. A trench coat blown by the wind trailed behind him. But there was no wind.

In that instant, Holloway knew that he was their man.

"Detective," a faraway feminine voice spoke to him.

Trent was in a trance, his concentration on the figure in black intense. Suddenly, the mourner who was not quite part of their group turned his head to the left, lifted his lapel pocket, and pulled a cigarette from it.

A flicker of green flame shot up from his lighter. Holloway could make out a portion of the man's face, but he would have no memory of it later.

You don't wanna be next, do you Trent?

The voice filled his mind, but it was not the feminine voice he heard a few moments ago. Trent instinctively knew the voice came from the man beside the tree.

After all, Trent, me and your old man knew you would

*be easy to get rid of. I mean, come on, you couldn't even
catch a football.*

"Detect…"

How could you miss that pass?

Holloway reluctantly broke the trance and found
Sheila tugging on the arm of his jacket. He looked at her,
then at the dispersing crowd.

He was standing in the pouring rain, soaked to the
bone.

"Honey, are you okay?" Sheila asked with worry as she
shielded him from the rain with her umbrella.

Holloway could not answer. Instead, he turned back to
the old oak tree but the man was no longer there.

"Hon…" Sheila said urgently.

Trent quickly composed himself. "I'm okay, I'm okay.
How long was I standing here?"

"Ten minutes at least. You saluted Heather in Jeremy's
honor and then you…you…"

"Zoned out?" Holloway finished her sentence.

"Yes. Exactly. You zoned out." Sheila was truly frightened. "I came over with the umbrella when it started to
rain but it was like you couldn't see or hear me."

"I'm sorry, Sheila. But I thought I saw something,"
Trent weakly tried to explain.

Holloway could not remember the man's face. But he
could not forget his words. *How did he know my name?*

The day after Jeremy Harris was laid to rest was
Halloween. The weather report said the temperature
would not reach above fifty degrees. So the mothers bun-

dled up their children with extra sweaters before sending them out to do their trick-or-treating. The curfew was still in effect, however, and the police shooed all the children back inside their homes with a sad 'Halloween is over, kids'. Officers were stationed on every corner from Main Street in Spring Garden to Calldown Boulevard in Shallow Front. The children were disappointed to tears and some families protested, but for the most part, people cooperated with the Mayor's plan. After all, it was a plan designed to keep them safe.

November swept in with rain and snow. The trees put themselves to rest. And as they rested, they dreamt of new leaves sprouting in the spring. But in Shallow Front, spring would be a long time coming.

Shallow Front almost canceled the Community Fair. The troupe from Texas traveled to states such as Virginia and Delaware. Every year between the third and the tenth of November, the troupe arrived with its rides and attractions and the town played host to visitors from as far away as Maryland, New Jersey and New York. As much as the city council objected, Mayor Nelson could not bring himself to sanction a move that would debilitate the town even worse. The high revenue the fair brought meant more security — not only in terms of finances but in terms of overtime for police officers patrolling the streets.

So when another murder took place, the town suffered badly. It happened the night the fair was being erected.

That evening, a man named Fred Stilton was setting

up a Funnel Cake stand. The temperature had dropped to thirty-eight degrees. Even so, Frank felt warm and cozy bundled in insulated coveralls. He decided to take a cigarette break and told his boss that he was going for a quick walk.

Fred walked over four miles. Harry Loughton discovered his body in a shallow creek.

During his walk, Fred apparently smoked only one cigarette. For a chain smoker, it seemed odd. The police found the soft pack and the remaining nineteen cigarettes strewn along the banks of the creek. Fred himself was found dead, face down in the water. It had frozen during the night and pulling Fred out had been difficult.

The Garrison City coroner determined that Fred had died of a heart attack. Although the authorities couldn't determine the cause of the heart attack, it was speculated that he died of fright.

Darla Goodman sipped from her glass of wine at Shaniqua's place even though she knew it wasn't good for the baby. With her other hand, she toyed with the small gold cross Frank Lion had given her. With it around her neck, she felt comforted and safe.

"I got a job," Shaniqua announced.

"Hey, that's great. Where at?" Darla asked.

"Town fair. It's only for a week, but after that I'm gonna drive down to Florida. I got some homies there. What about you?" she asked.

"Don't know," Darla said. "I've been looking just about everywhere but no one's hiring."

"Did you tell Frank?" Shaniqua suddenly changed the subject.

"Tell him what?" Darla asked then realized what her friend was talking about. "Oh. The pregnancy. Yes, I told him. He didn't really say much." She tilted her head back and downed the last of her wine. Her large hoop earrings swung back and forth on her ear lobes.

This time Darla changed the subject. "I never went back to Gussby's, not even to pick up my last check."

"Why not?" Shaniqua asked.

"Would you go back there after what happened to Billy Warrington?"

"Good point." In fact Shaniqua hadn't gone back to Gussby's either.

"Next time I see Frank, I think I'm gonna tell him how much I love him. I mean. I know he's married and all, but I can't help feeling the way I do," Darla confessed.

"Girl, you are playing with fire, you know th-"

"I don't care, Shaniqua. Really. I would do anything for him."

If you believe, and I believe, what else is there to worry about? Frank had said.

Chapter 7

Cotton candy began to spin the first day of the Shallow Front Festival. A little girl with pigtails jumped up and down as she was handed the long paper cone topped with a sticky pink pillow.

"Here you go, kiddo," the Tidbie Cotton Candy man said as he took a dollar bill from the girl's father.

On the far side of the field, a colorful Ferris wheel looped round and round and all the childrens' favorite roller coaster, The Gut Buster, rattled on its steel rails. Clowns danced between the rows of food stands and games of chance as many people milled about enjoying the festivities.

Frank Lion and his family were among the crowd. His children ran in front of him as his wife monitored from his side. Frank wondered how long he had before Deb found out about his affair with Darla.

The smell of peanuts, cotton candy and soft pretzels did little to conceal the fact that old man winter was coming. And even less to assuage Frank Lion's guilt.

People came to the festival from all over — Lincoln, Spring Garden, Harper. The owner of the Arliss Hotel handed out free hot chocolate to those unprepared for the sharply colder weather. And every street corner was blocked off, though no one really noticed.

The serial killer stood alone in the shadows. His desire to find her became a painful longing in his loins. To distract himself, he contemplated the eradication of all cops and of all peacemakers. *Why not?* It was finally time for his coming out party.

I see her, he thought as he stood in the alley between the bank and the deli. He smelled her over the sweet stench of caramel popcorn and funnel cakes. She had been seeded and was now tainted. If the woman was carrying him inside of her, he would take care of it.

The killer felt himself grow hard and hot. He bit the inside of his lower lip and rocked hard on his dress shoes. The moment was as exciting for him now as it had been the night he murdered Cassandra Evans.

He watched as the tall woman walked toward the pay phone on Second Street. Dusk had settled over the town and night approached. His favorite time of day. The stranger who disemboweled women and eerily infected men with the flu silently stood silhouetted against the transitional sky.

Do you see what eye see?

The woman made her phone call. He watched as she rocked her hips back and forth. He liked the way she moved, in sync with the way he rocked in his shoes. The colorful lights from the Ferris wheel shone in his bright, black eyes. He tightened his fists in his pockets and bit his lip until blood poured from the corners of his mouth. The moment was upon him.

Then voices very near nudged him back to the present.

He turned his head toward the sound and quickly, he ducked into the darkness.

A second later, several teenagers passed near enough to where the killer was hiding that he could have reached out and touched them.

I almost came, the killer thinks.

The woman finished her phone call and sat alone on a nearby bench. The man who was the talk of the town crept up behind her very slowly and noiselessly. The woman turned around but it was too late.

The man who had snapped Jessica Frommel's neck grabbed her by the throat and pulled her away from the crowd. His nails dug into the soft skin of her neck. Pure terror prevented her from screaming as he pulled her into the park.

"Tell me your name," he demanded.

The woman was too frightened to speak but the killer already knew that she was not the one.

Blood leaked from her neck between his thick fingers as he dug his nails deeper and deeper into her flesh.

The woman tried to speak but only gurgles emerged from the back of her throat. She was drowning in her own blood. He was crushing her windpipe. Blood spurted out of her nose and mouth.

"I can hear your heart skipping," the killer said.

The woman's eyes widened in terror.

"It is sweet, sweet music to my ears, lovely."

The stranger pulled the woman closer. She smelled his breath and his horrid scent. Before she passed out, she had the strangest thought. *I smell burning matches.*

The Shallow Front serial killer ripped off her left ear

with his mouth. Stunned back to consciousness by the excruciating pain, the woman stared into his evil eyes, captivated by their hypnotic terror and a madness that could never be described in words. She tried again to scream. She was rewarded with a slash to her right breast with his concealed straight razor.

He pulled her deeper into the park. Groups of revelers frolicked in the night mere feet away from where the attacker hacked away at his victim. No one noticed a bloody woman struggling for her life, trying to scream for help. Unable to speak, she begged for mercy in her mind, screamed it to him, never knowing that the man heard her thoughts of mercy and enjoyed every thoughtful scream.

Her body would be found the following morning, another mystery that would baffle police. This murder, however, was special and would forever change what would be the future of Shallow Front.

Chapter 8

Very early Sunday morning, a heavy fog rolled in as a crew began to dismantle the fairground rides and stands. Harry Loughton drove up in his old pickup truck. His headlights reflected off the white mist and created phantoms shapes that resembled ghosts. Roy, his big old lab, sat next to him on the bench seat sniffing the heavy air out the passenger side window.

Harry had been having his troubles sleeping ever since that night at Gussby's. It bothered him that Billy Warrington and he had that confrontation and kept thinking that maybe Billy wouldn't have killed himself if they hadn't.

Nightmare was a word Harry never had to use because he never had a bad dream in his life. Lately, though, every time he crawled into bed, he fell deeply asleep almost instantly and dreamed the most horrible dreams.

SHALLOW FRONT CEMETERY. The rusted sign hung crooked on the fence next to the rusted gate. In his dreams, Harry knew what was beyond the gate, a graveyard. But he pushed the squeaky gate open anyway and stepped onto the brick path that led to the main road.

By all accounts, Harry was not a man easily frightened. The cemetery in his dreams, however, petrified him, yet he walked deeper into the graveyard. Tombstones jutted out of the ground like jagged teeth and Harry felt as if he was trapped in the jaws of a monstrous beast.

Harry walked on, remembering the days of his youth when he had brought his teenage girlfriends to fornicate in the mausoleum, the little house that was home to a family of dead. He never worried about them objecting to his adolescent fervor and the girls he brought never seemed to mind fucking in a crypt. It was fun. Harry tried to call up those old memories to help calm him But he couldn't. Fear grew in the pit of his stomach and knew its roots but was powerless to stop the momentum.

The last headstone on his left had fallen to the ground. And as Harry had done every time in this recurring dream, walked over to it knowing that he would see the gaping hole in the ground where a body once rested.

Very carefully, Harry peered into the black hole that went deeper than the meager light revealed.

There was nothing inside.

He gingerly stepped around the black pit and stood over the gravestone.

HERE LIES WILLIAM (BILLY) WARRINGTON.

The edge of the stone that had been in the ground was caked with dirt and grass. Several slimy worms wiggled around in the mess.

Billy was dead. He slit his own throat from ear to ear right in front of everyone at Gussby's. So why was his grave empty?

So he can do it again Harry suddenly thought, *this time*

to me.

"NO!" Harry shouted. "NO, DEAR GOD! NO!!!"

Off to his left, there was a rustling in the hedges and Harry saw a figure slip into the woods.

"WHO IS THAT?" Harry screamed.

But there would never be a response.

Harry would wake up then, sometimes sobbing but always wondering where his sanity had gone. Had old age reminded him that he would soon be in a grave of his own?

The fairgrounds were barely visible from where Harry sat with Roy. He couldn't see much through the fog but knew that the workers were dismantling the Ferris wheel. Harry was glad they were going. He didn't like the fair much.

With a stick match, he lit an old corncob pipe packed with sweet cherry tobacco and watched as the smoke swirled out the window and mingled with the fog. He grabbed a black plastic garbage bag from behind the seat and stepped out of the truck. Roy jumped out after him.

The two walked slowly toward the ruined fairgrounds. It would be a good night for picking up recyclable cans and bottles to turn in at the Foodway. Roy trotted ahead and sniffed out a half eaten hot dog.

Harry stopped for a moment, puffed on his pipe and bundled his jacket around him as a rush of cold air slapped him across the face. A long winter was coming for sure.

By the park bench, Harry scooped up three soda cans.

He noticed that the pay phone was dangling off the hook, swinging as if alive in the crisp breeze. Loughton ambled over to it and replaced the phone onto the receiver. Not too far away, Roy started to bark.

Harry turned. Only Roy's back half was visible in the patch of fog that apparently caught his attention. His bushy tail fanned back and forth and he barked again. Then suddenly, he yelped, jumped out of the mist and ran to his master.

"What's the matta, old boy?" Harry asked. Roy stuck by his master's side as Harry walked over to where his dog had been. Roy lowered his head and sniffed the ground again. Harry followed his dog's nose until it stopped over a patch of grass. Upon closer inspection, Harry saw what Roy had been barking at.

A human hand.

"Oh, Jesus," Harry swore. His pipe fell from his lips as he stumbled backwards. Yet he could not take his eyes off the hand.

His gaze followed the fingers to the palm and then up the arm and then on to the rest of the body. Instinctively, Harry's hand went up to his mouth. He was shaking so badly, he could hardly remain on his feet.

Then the pay phone rang.

Harry almost had a heart attack. He struggled to regain his balance. He spotted the pay phone and focused on it as it rang a second time. The fog had thickened and lingered like ghosts. At that moment, the world felt very surreal to Harry. But he was aware of one fact. He and Roy were all alone. The partygoers had gone home to their locked doors and windows hours ago. And the fair workers were too far away to be of any help. It took all his strength to take a step toward the pay phone.

Harry tried to calm his nerves. *Wrong number is all...* Harry thought.

"Hello?"

Nothing.

"Hello?"

Again no sound came from the caller but he was still on the line. Harry decided it would be better to not know who was on the other end and was about to hang up when he heard a voice.

"Your sickness has cleared up quite fine, old man."

The voice sounded like a record playing on a slow turntable. And underneath it, Harry thought he heard something that sounded like a blazing fire.

"Wh-who is this?" he demanded with as much confidence as he could muster.

"Who do you think it is? Better yet, who do you want it to be?" the voice asked as if a thousand rusty nails were lodged in its throat.

"I don't know what the hell this is, but if-if you're th-th...," Harry couldn't manage the rest.

"But I am, dear boy. I am the one indeed. Like how she looks?"

"Tell me who you are, you son of a bitch!"

"Speak that way to me again, Harry, and you'll find yourself alive and kicking in that deep, black hole you're always dreaming about."

Harry reeled. *How does he know my name and how the hell does he know about my dreams?*

"I know a lot, Harry," said the voice on the other end of

the phone in answer to Harry's silent question. "I am the reason Billy killed himself and someday, I will be the reason for your death as well."

The caller cackled insanely. Harry screamed over it.

"I'm calling the police, you son of a bitch! They're gonna find you and when they do...."

"They already haaave, Harry," the voice taunted.

A long silence followed as Harry stared at the receiver in his hand.

"See ya around, Harry," the killer at last said.

Harry dropped the phone.

As quickly as he could, he rushed to his pickup truck, the few cans in the black bag long forgotten. He locked the doors after letting Roy in and drove away as fast as he could. He called the police only after he was safe in his house.

Detective Holloway was asleep in his bed when his pager sounded. He leaned over with eyes half closed and checked the caller ID. It didn't take him long to recognize the precinct's number and call it back.

"Spring Garden Police," a female voice answered.

"Yes, this is Detective Trent Holloway. I was paged."

"Which department, sir?"

"Homicide," he replied.

"One moment," the desk officer said as she placed him on hold. Holloway paced the kitchen floor in the dark as he waited. He reached up to the top of the refrigerator and grabbed a pack of cigarettes. He shook one out and was lighting it when the officer returned on the line.

"Sir, are you still there?"

"Of course I am," Holloway replied with little patience.

"Yes, sir. I'll connect you to Captain Pullman."

Pullman? Holloway thought. Already his stomach began to ache. He feared the worst, that the serial killer had struck again. What else could be so important at a quarter to three in the morning?

"Trent, this is Pullman. Sorry to wake you."

"No problem. What's going on?" Trent asked already knowing the answer.

"He struck again..." Pullman started.

Holloway opened and closed the refrigerator door open and fanned himself with the cool air. He didn't know how much more he could take.

"Where's the body, Captain?" Holloway asked as he exhaled white smoke.

"Downtown Shallow Front near Nolan Avenue. Harry Loughton found her. Says he went there to get a few cans after the fair, like he does every year. He called us after he got home. Lion is already on his way. I need you there, too, Trent."

"Okay. I'm on it," Trent replied and hung up the phone.

He dressed in a hurry and cut his way through the fog. The temperature had fallen and it was very cold.

When he reached the crime scene, he saw that Lion had had the area cordoned off with the familiar yellow crime scene tape. Two police cars flooded the dark streets with flashing red and blue lights. Sergeant Lion stood within the protected area with his head lowered. Two patrolmen were closing the streets to the traffic that was sure to arrive as soon as the sun came up.

Holloway approached Detective Frank Lion. Both men wore disheveled tan trench coats. Both men looked haggard. But something was especially wrong with Lion.

Holloway stopped beside him, shoulder to shoulder, and looked down at what his colleague was looking at. Another naked young woman had been butchered. The victim's left breast had been severed from her body. Tassels of bloody veins were strewn across her arm. Her left ear was missing. And her chest had been torn wide open. Holloway saw that her attacker had taken the time to remove her heart. He had done that very carefully. Just like how he had taken Jessica Frommel's eyes.

It would take fingerprinting, however, to identify this new victim. In addition to her heart, the murdering madman had taken her face. He had skinned her down to bare skull.

Frank Lion already knew who the woman was. She was wearing the cross he had given her around her neck.

"Why do you think the fucker took her heart?" Holloway asked. He was breathing heavily, a handkerchief over his mouth. Holloway was truly terrified. He turned to Lion who had not taken his eyes off the victim.

"Detective..." Holloway started.

Detective Lion could not respond. All he could think was *my sweet Darla.* The sudden spasm of goose flesh that crawled up his back parted the hairs on his neck.

He thought about the serial killer who had murdered the woman he secretly loved.

No one of the police knew the victim was pregnant with his child. And the awful truth was that Lion could not tell his colleagues. The consequences would be disastrous. His marriage would be over for sure and with it, his life. Frank was disgusted with himself for his selfishness and guilt.

He had made love to Darla and comforted her when she needed it most. He told her everything would be fine. He lied.

He told her things even his wife didn't even know, secrets of his heart.

And then they shared the ultimate secret. Her baby. His baby.

Tears streamed down Detective Lion's cheeks. He hoped that Holloway wouldn't notice. But Holloway noticed everything.

His baby...

Holloway stared at the detective's face. Lion remained embedded in thought.

If we have faith, we can do anything

Frank Lion could do nothing more than cry.

"Frank..." Holloway started.

"Can you imagine how scared she must have been?" Frank asked as if he was talking to himself.

"Frank?" Holloway implored.

"Where's her heart, Trent? Huh? Where's her fucking heart!!!" Lion screamed before turning and walking away, Holloway followed.

"Frank, what the hell is wrong with you?"

"Nothing, dammit. I-I just can't believe we can't catch this motherfucker." Detective Lion rubbed his flattop like he always did when he was nervous or thinking. "We've decoded everything, ran every test. We even put on extra patrols. Hell, we've involved the best crime lab in the world. And they're clueless!"

"Frank, don't do this to yo..." Holloway began.

"And you know what else?" Frank interjected. "What kind of serial killer avoids getting nabbed for this long, huh?" Frank needed an excuse for his real frustration, which was Darla. At that moment, Frank was a mere shell, empty, yet filled with grief the size of a knot on that hundred year old oak tree.

At that moment, Trent didn't understand Frank but knew to tread lightly. "We're doing everything we can, Detective," Holloway said as gently as possible.

Frank looked around and realized he had ended up in the middle of the street. He was filled with a seething hatred that both startled and scared him.

After a brief moment of silence, Holloway said, "We better go back over there, Frank." He had never known Frank to act like this, not in all the fifteen years they'd worked together.

"I'll be there in a minute, Trent," Frank replied.

"Sure. Take your time," Holloway said.

Trent returned to the crime scene to find Betty Samus, the forensics trainee who worked on the Cassandra Evans case.

"We meet again, Betty," Holloway said in a friendly manner.

Betty was all business. "You better take a look at this,

sir." Her grim eyes gave away her feelings.

As Holloway watched, Betty plucked a bloody piece of paper with her tweezers from the crook of the victim's elbow. Holloway pulled on a pair of latex gloves before taking the note from her. It smelled of burnt matches.

"We've already lifted prints off of it," Betty said.

"Like it matters," Holloway mumbled and then turned his full attention to the note. Within the circle of light from his flashlight, Holloway read:

The sin that lies within tells the truth in its own womb. So slice my wrists to see what this world has left for me...

"What the hell does that mean?" Holloway asked out loud. He handed the note back to Betty, took out his notebook and wrote down the words exactly so he would remember them later. Betty found the proper size plastic evidence bag and slid the note inside.

"You want copies, sir?" Betty said.

"Yeah. Better make me copies, Betty. Thanks."

The forensics team lifted the dead woman and placed her gently on a body bag. Frank Lion watched as they zipped it closed.

Down in the quicksand, this time to stay. Forever.

Two days after she was found, the woman was identified as Darla Goodman.

Chapter 9

Detton Holloway was helping his daddy shovel snow. It was the first real snow of the year. Great big flakes like angel ashes fell from the grayest sky Shallow Front had seen that year.

"Build a snowman, daddy!" little Detton cried as he tried to pack the snow into a ball.

"In a while, little man. Daddy's got to shovel the driveway first before Pastor Kline comes over," Trent shouted back to his son.

Holloway had invited the pastor for dinner as he did every year. In better times, Trent would have coached little league with the pastor. But things hadn't been very good for a long while.

At five forty-five, Pastor William Kline pulled into the Holloway's freshly shoveled driveway. Trent waited for him at the front door.

"Pastor, how are you?"

"Fine, fine. And how are you, Detective?"

"I've been better, William," Holloway replied as he took the Pastor's coat. "Make yourself comfortable. Sheila made a meatloaf."

"Well, that wife of yours has quite a memory. Meatloaf

is one of my favorite dishes. My wife used to make it," Pastor Kline said with sadness in his eyes. "I miss her so much sometimes. But the good Lord saw fit to take her to a better place."

Holloway smiled compassionately and squeezed the his friend's shoulder. Sheila was in the kitchen, mashing potatoes, when he entered.

"The pastor is here, hon..." Trent abruptly stopped speaking when he saw the look on his wife's face. Her little kitchen television was on.

"I'm pretty sure this is not a good time, but it's all over the news," Sheila said and nodded in the direction of the Channel 6 broadcast.

"What is?" Holloway asked.

"Well, the press is chewing out the Spring Garden police force up and spitting it out. It's blasphemy, if you ask me," Sheila said as she mashed the potatoes with extra fervor.

Holloway wasn't upset. "People can talk all they want. We've done everything by the book. We have a serial killer, killing pregnant women, for a still unknown reason, no motiva..."

Holloway turned and saw that Pastor Kline had joined them in the kitchen. The look on his face was very serious. "Are you talking about the same man who somehow uses the dead's fingerprints?" he asked.

"Yes," Holloway grimaced. "I've tried not to think about it too much, though, because I've been told by the FBI to not give too much credit to that line of thought. They keep saying is it isn't possible."

"But it must be possible, Trent, because it's happening," Pastor Kline pointed out.

"You're right. It sure is." Holloway poured himself and the Pastor a glass of wine.

"What are the police going to do now? I certainly hope not what they've been doing," Kline asked.

"There isn't much we can do, William. We've boosted security and enforced the curfew. Somehow the sick bastard, excuse my French, has managed to get past all of the extra precautions. We have over twenty state patrol cars out there helping us right now. That's in addition to our own resources." Trent took a gulp of wine to help calm his nerves. A headache was brewing at his temples.

"Here we go guys!" Sheila announced and ushered them into the dining room. As she set the dinner down on the table, she smiled sadly at William.

"Always a pleasure," he said.

Detton joined them at the table, the blush of cold air still visible on his pink cheeks.

"Well then, shall we say grace?" William asked. They bowed their heads and closed their eyes as Pastor Kline led them in prayer.

"We thank you, Lord, for the sustenance that you have placed before us to help keep us happy and healthy. We also ask you, Lord, to help end the tyranny that has fallen upon this great land, a tyranny that is unable to leave well enough alone. And we pray for an answer in Jesus' name. Amen."

"Say, Trent, you think someday soon before it gets to covered with snow that you could come down to the church and help me with the oak tree that fell, you know, that stump I mentioned? I can't remember if I asked you before or not."

"You have," Holloway said, "and I will."

"Thank you. Harry and I tried to move it but the darn roots are still attached, and we couldn't budge it. I need a young man with an even stronger back to help me."

"You give me too much credit, William. But I'll see what I can do," Holloway said with a smile.

After Pastor Kline left that evening, Trent stood alone on his porch and watched as the wind lifted the snow up and spun it out into the night. The moon was full and the ground glowed eerily in the twilight. Sheila tucked Detton into bed then joined her husband outside.

"He asleep?"

"Sure is. Playing in the snow is the one sure way to exhaust him," Sheila said with a warm smile. "You should be exhausted, too."

"I know. But I can't sleep," Holloway said. "I have a lot on my mind." In truth, all he could think about was Frank and how devastated he was when he looked down at the victim. It was as if Frank had known her.

"I think we should do something this weekend. Just you and me. You need a break, Trent. This madness, this, this shit is so terrible. You need to get away from it for a while." Sheila rarely cursed and when she did, Trent knew she was serious.

"I don't know, Sheila," Trent replied weakly.

"Well, I do know. Let's go to the Arliss this weekend. We'll take Detton to my mother's." Sheila's mind was made up.

Holloway snuffed his cigarette out in the snow. "You're right, as usual. It sounds like a good idea."

Trent followed his wife inside and hugged her, leaving the cold behind, if just for a little while.

During the night, another four inches of snow fell. School was cancelled, and Sheila let her son sleep in under the canopy of toys hanging from his ceiling. Trent took advantage of his day off and snuggled with his wife. When he woke up at ten, he heard Detton giggling at his cartoons. After breakfast, he promised his son an afternoon of sledding at Carson Park.

Twenty miles away, at the rundown Biar Apartments near Gussby's, Shaniqua Holmes shoveled snow. Her back was already throbbing with a dull pain, and she had a long way to go. The snow was deep and heavy, but she was glad to be the one holding the shovel for a change. *Sometimes you're the one holding the shovel, and sometimes you're under it,* she thought.

"Jesus, Darla," Shaniqua sighed. Her heart felt heavy, the weight of her sorrow engulfed her. Darla had been her friend. There would be no more late nights passing stories back and forth over glasses of cheap red wine. There would be no more talk of Frank Lion and her future and his secrets. They would be locked away forever in the deep chamber of her missing heart.

Darla had seen something that night.

Shaniqua paused in her shoveling.

My friend saw someone, or something, standing across the street.

Before she threw the next pile of snow, Shaniqua stopped to gather her strength. She thought about Florida and of how long she might stay there and how she would try to get her life together and... Darla.

Darla never mentioned anything about the thing across the street, but Shaniqua knew Darla had seen something because her dreams told her so.

In her dreams, a tall man with black eyes wearing an equally black broad brimmed hat held one end of a shiny chain leash in his hand. The other end was wrapped around the neck of the biggest wolf she has ever seen.

I know what he looks like. He's the killer, yes. If only I could remember.

Shaniqua threw more snow over her shoulder and tried to remember. The chill that crawled up her spine made no attempt to conceal its origins. Shaniqua was very afraid.

Impulsively, she tossed the shovel into the pile of snow she had just made, went inside and packed up her few meager possessions in an old suitcase. Then, checking her back every few minutes, Shaniqua walked to the Main Street bus station.

"Fuck the snow," was the last thing she ever said in Shallow Front.

Trent did as he promised and took Detton sledding. Wearing a snow cap and five o'clock shadow, he bundled up his son in a blue snowsuit, striped wool hat and thick mittens. He grabbed the toboggan from the garage and loaded it in his pickup truck.

With a hot cup of coffee in the cup holder and a cigarette in his hand, Trent drove slowly to Carson Park. Instead of thinking about the outing, his thoughts were consumed by the strange note the killer left with his fourth victim.

Slice your wrists to see what this world has left for me.

Unknowingly, Trent pulled into the same parking space Jeremy Harris had the day he was killed.

Suddenly, he felt miserable. He sat in his car and felt utterly useless as a policeman, as a homicide detective. The cases depleted his confidence and made him question everything he believed about himself.

"Daddy?" Trent felt a tug on his sleeve. "You swedding, daddy?" Detton asked.

"No buddy. You go ahead. I'll watch from right here," Trent replied.

"Kay!" Detton laughed, running with the toboggan up the hill. He came sliding down fast. Holloway laughed.

"That was great! Do it again!"

Holloway turned and saw the giant cross towering into the cold winter sky. In his peripheral vision, he noticed people leaving the park. He saw the changes in the townspeople. No one trusted anymore. People locked their doors and tucked their children in bed early every night. Guns remained loaded. And afraid of becoming pregnant, women pushed their lovers away. There wasn't much love in Shallow Front these days, Trent sadly thought.

"YAAAAAAAHY!" Detton yelled with glee. Holloway turned to watch his son slide down the hill again. He laughed as he went, and as quickly as the ride was over,

Detton was back at the top of the hill ready to go again. Trent leaned against his truck and lit another cigarette. He realized in that moment that as harsh as the world had become, he was fortunate to have his family, his son.

They were worth dying for.

Snow fell as the Anti-Christ walked along Mill Street. He continued his search.

In the still night, his long black trench coat billowed around him like a flag caught in a strong breeze. The delicate white flakes sizzled to steam as they landed on his broad shoulders. And with every step he took, the snow beneath his feet melted.

As he scanned the night, the dark black of his eyes was gone, and in its place was the white reflection from the fresh snow. Without irises, he looked completely mad.

He noticed the dead trees buried under blankets of white and smiled to himself. *Death*, he thought. His nostrils flared, and he grinned in delight with teeth so incredibly white they appeared to be fake, as if they belonged to someone else.

And they did.

He landed in this town at the end of last summer but would soon have to continue his search elsewhere. So sad. Willie Zigs did not live up to expectations, and the killer had no choice but to leave. He had sensed pure evil inside of Willie and it made him giddy. He thought he could use it to his advantage. But Willie was stupid. *He couldn't even dodge the bullet I told him was coming his way!*

Cassandra Evans murdered by Willie Zigs. It would have been perfect. But then he was forced to take her himself. He smelled it in her. She was tainted.

Up in the mountains near that shabby little place called Lincoln, he had smelled it on the Dawson girl as well. He took care of it, though, as she thought about urinating in the woods. He took care of her like he took care of all of them. Always like the last time, the last time, the last time, the last time.

As he passed by the Shallow Front police station, he laughed. *Here I am. Come and get me,* he thought. But they would never figure it out.

So when he looked up into the night, the Anti-Christ smiled and said a silent prayer.

Dear father. Thank you for casting me out of your boring shelter and into the depths I now dwell. You think you know how it ends. Well, I can assure you it will not end that way. This is only the beginning. So hide him from me. You do it so well. I am the wolf among the meek sheep of this city. And they will tremble for as long as I wish.

Trent and Sheila checked into the Arliss Hotel the next afternoon.

After they settled in, Trent took off his shoes and stretched out across the bed. Sheila soon joined him and they remained there the rest of the afternoon. The only time they ventured out was after the maid, Sister, delivered their service. Sheila went to get some ice for her wine.

When she returned to the room, Trent had turned on the news.

"Honey," Sheila implored, "we came here to get away from all of that. Turn off the TV, please."

Trent ignored her. The ten o'clock local news had just started, and Trent watched as photos of Darla Goodman popped up on the screen. The handsome newscaster reported the details of her murder from the crime scene and concluded his broadcast with the fact that Darla was pregnant, just like the other victims.

Holloway shuddered. *All those unborn children.* The serial killer was targeting pregnant women, and Trent didn't know why. *Why?* his mind screamed. *What was the significance? Surely by now Captain Pullman did not believe that it was all coincidence.*

Trent could not stop thinking about the cases. The note found on Darla's body frustrated him in particular. He felt it was a warning.

Slice my wrists to see what this world has left for me.

Then he realized that the note was about suicide. *Whose?* he asked himself. *And why would someone commit suicide?*

The answer was far more complicated than he knew.

Chapter 10

At seven-thirty in the morning, before Trent and Sheila Holloway left for the Arliss Hotel, Frank Lion woke to the aroma of bacon, eggs and fresh coffee. His stomach told him to get out of bed.

As he stood up, his head hurt badly. He had spent most the night crying. Deb Lion had fallen asleep next to him unaware that he was crying over the death of his lover. Frank had told her that work stress and all the deaths contributed to his frustration, fear and anger. Frank was used to telling lies.

He missed Darla. He had truly loved her. Other than his mother, she was the only woman who ever really understood him. And she was gone.

Lion wanted to believe that he would go to her little trailer and that she would greet him with her warm smile and a hug. But he didn't want to think about that, couldn't think about that. Because when he thought about physical contact with her, his heart broke. The killer took her child, his child.

And Mikey. Frank could not think about him either. The little boy was so confused and frightened when they took him away to the orphanage. He only wanted his mother. But she wouldn't ever be here again. She would never see him graduate high school or get married. And she would never again tell him again how much she loved him. Mikey would never know more about her than he did now, and Lion grieved for both of them.

Murder was abrupt and never rational. Michael would be confused for years to come.

Besides Michael, Darla had nothing when she died except the hope to someday be with Frank.

Frank couldn't think about that either. He hated himself for the weakness he couldn't control and for feeling grateful that he would never have to deal with the birth of his child and the consequences of his actions. Deb would never know what went on in the little trailer that Darla could barely heat. The detective was grateful that his family would not be torn apart by Darla's child.

Frank hated himself for many reasons yet he selfishly remained alone in the darkness of his bedroom praying to God to bring Darla back even as Deb called him to eat the breakfast she cooked just for him. *God.* An entity Frank did not believe in and never would.

When he finally did stand up, he dressed for work in his good pants and white shirt. To his surprise, a piece of paper fell out of his pants pocket and onto the carpet.

At first, Frank believed it was the note forensics found in Darla's mouth. He kept a copy for his personal vendetta against the psychopath. But the note he held in his hand was from Darla.

Dear Frank,
I hope the next time I see you, you will hold me the same

way you held me tonight.

Every night before I go to sleep, I hold the cross you gave me in my hands, and pray for us to be together.

I am sorry I have nothing to give you because I am so poor. I hope my love will be enough.

Love always,

Darla

Frank read the note quickly. Then he read it again more slowly. Thoughts of Darla shadowed his mind, and he sobbed tears of angry sorrow.

Why would God let a man like that exist? Because there is no God.

Frank fell back on the bed. Holding his head in his hands as he cried, Darla's letter fluttered slowly to the floor like a feather caught in the wind.

The front door opened and closed. Frank realized that his wife had left for work.

And if you believe and I believe....

Frank stepped from the darkness of his bedroom into the sunny living room. He made his way to the kitchen where his breakfast waited for him on the table.

What do we have to worry about?

He noticed a slip of paper was tucked under his plate of bacon and eggs. When he pulled it out, he saw that it was written in red ink the color of Darla's lipstick.

Hey Frank,

I know you are feeling pretty down but don't worry. You'll catch the guy.

If you wouldn't mind, could you tie up the old magazines in the basement and put them out on the curb?

There's a lot of them by the water heater.
Love, Deb

Another note, but Frank didn't like this one at all. He knew his wife inside and out. Deb didn't give two shits about how he felt. She wanted those magazines out. Period. And what Deb wanted and needed always came first. If he tried to reason with her, it was like trying to reason with a block of stone. She wouldn't budge.

"Yeah right, hon. Whatever you want, hon," he said disdainfully as he tossed his breakfast in the trash.

Frank had no intention of doing what his wife had asked. Instead, he grabbed a bottle of aspirins from the cabinet over the sink and twisted the cap off a bottle of beer. He washed the pills down with a gulp and decided to grab the rest of the six-pack he bought the day before. Frank's children had left with their mother who would school them in between phone calls and appointments. She home schooled both of them in her office.

"Suck the wet end," he said aloud and poured more beer down his throat.

Frank walked over to the basement door and swung it open. The ancient wooden stairs down to the basement stared back at him. He had promised to fix the cracked ones years ago but never got around to. His wife never missed an opportunity to berate him.

"You're so lazy," he said mocking his wife's voice. "You always say you'll fix'em but you never do. You never do anything I ask you to do."

"Why don't you do this, my dear?" Frank asked as he reached inside his pants. "Why don't you reach in, pull out my snake and help it shed its skin, hmmmm? How'bout you do that, my sweet?"

Frank pulled the chain on the light and in the brightness, felt ridiculous that he had been yelling at no one.

"Oh, my Darla, my sweet sweeeeet Darla," Frank started to sing. On an empty stomach, the beer had no problem finding its way to his brain. The singing cheered him up and took away some of the sting of reality. Deb's note was still in his hand. He crumpled it and tossed his reality somewhere in the basement.

As he went down the stairs, each step crackled under him. It was noticeably colder in the basement, but Frank didn't mind. *You know,* he said to himself, *I kind of like it down here.*

Every corner was shrouded in cobwebs and boxes of Deb's stuff crowded most of the floor space. An old ironing board stood open in the middle of the main area and empty wine bottles lay all about. A moth-eaten green army jacket hung on a hook, and old framed prints of Greece and Athens were crusted with flourishing mold.

Who will paint for me?

Brilliant sunlight shone through a box-shaped window at the far end of the basement. Frank saw the snow against the glass.

"Yippity, yippity," he said aloud and finished his beer.

Around the other side of the stairs was dark and dusty. The water heater was almost covered with old magazines and newspapers, fishing guides, tour guides, realtor guides, old telephone books stacked against it.

"This shit ain't mine," Frank said to no one as he flipped through the pile.

Old porno magazines. "Okay. Maybe some of this stuff is mine," he said with a chuckle.

Frank picked up a copy with a mostly naked blonde on the cover and flipped through it. Dust puffed up in the air and dappled the sunlight. He was mesmerized by the effect.

He stared at the dust speckling the wedge of sunlight coming through the window. His eyes were devoid of all emotion, but on the inside, Frank was despondent. Thoughts of Darla swam around in his mind.

He grabbed two boxes of magazines and pulled them into the sunlight. He sat down and read through some of the older ones. By the time he was finished, he was crying.

Sighing, he wiped his shirt sleeve across his face. Frank could barely stand the pain he felt. He hung his head in sorrow. A single tear rolled down his cheek.

When he looked up, he noticed a metal object glimmering on the ironing board.

Frank squinted at it and approached the object slowly. He had not noticed it before. On closer inspection, he saw that it was a straight razor.

How did this get here? he asked himself. *Why does Deborah own a straight razor?*

Must be her father's, he thought.

No. That's not right, Her sister got all of dad's stuff after he died of cancer last year.

Frank looked down at it with red eyes. He felt weak and vulnerable.

The razor is brand fucking new!!!!!!

He grabbed the handle. There were no carvings or

markings on it. No initials indicating who it belonged to so Frank claimed it as his own. *Finders keepers, loosers weepers.* He smiled.

The straight razor's handle was rimmed with gold and very shiny. It sparkled even in the dim basement light. Frank opened the blade and thought about his own father who used to shave with one just like it. It was sleek, smooth and very sharp.

"Now why didn't I see this thing down here before?" he said out loud. His voice echoed hollowly off the basement walls.

"Oh, well," he sighed, placing the straight razor back on the ironing board and grabbing the two boxes of his old magazines. He brought them upstairs and onto the front porch.

Let Deb take her own shit to the curb, he thought.

Back inside, Frank whistled and went to his bedroom, reappearing with a pair of old jeans and a stained white t-shirt folded under his arm. He went back down into the basement and began to undress. All the while he sang "Darla, my sweet Darla. You're more than a friend to me eee eeee eeee."

Naked, he folded his good clothes and placed them on the ironing board. Then he dressed in his old jeans and t-shirt.

Frank went to the darkest corner of the basement and sat down in between the water heater and the cement block wall. The sunlight didn't reach him.

The water heater kicked on and off every twenty minutes or so and kept Frank company with its steady hum. He flicked his new straight razor open and closed as he sat in the dark. Frank smiled and whistled every so often and listened to the water heater click on and off, on and off, on and off.

Time passed but Frank wouldn't have been able to say how long he had been sitting there even if he was in his right mind. And he most definitely was not in his right mind.

Frank Lion asked no one, "Tell me what it is that you want."

He cocked his head to the side as if listening to a response. Then in one swift motion, he brought the razor down fast and sliced through the skin, muscles and veins of his right wrist.

The blade was so sharp, the slit didn't start to bleed for a moment which gave him plenty of time to slash his left wrist.

Frank dropped the straight razor and it clattered to the floor. Then the flood gates opened. His blood ran in rivers down his fingers and pooled on the floor in front of him. He watched with detached fascination as his life leaked out of him. For a few minutes, before he lost consciousness, he watched as the magazines and cardboard boxes soaked up the warm sticky liquid like giant blotters. Frank Lion slumped to the floor and fell face first into his own blood. He thought of his wife and children. And of Darla. Dear, sweet beautiful Darla. It was a sin to commit suicide, punishable by a trip to hell. Frank didn't think once about hell.

But hell was thinking about him.

So slice my wrists to see what the world has left for me.

Chapter 11

Trent Holloway was paged in his hotel room at eight o'clock the next morning. The little square pager vibrated itself off the night table and fell to the floor. Trent wanted to throw it out the window, but instead he read the number and dialed it. Precinct 3, Captain Pullman. Again.

"Captain, what's up?" Trent asked when Pullman got on the line.

"You're never gonna believe this, Trent," his captain said.

"What now?" Trent asked, dreading what was to come next.

"Frank Lion is dead," Pullman told him flatly.

Holloway almost dropped the phone. "H-ho-how?" Trent managed to ask in trembling voice.

"He committed suicide, Trent. Yesterday morning. He went into this basement, crawled between the water heater and the wall and sliced his wrists."

"Jesus...oh my God," a stunned Detective Holloway exclaimed.

"I've got something else to tell you, too."

"What's that, Captain?"

"We found a note in Frank's pants pocket from Darla Goodman. Apparently, Detective Lion was having an affair with her."

"What's the matter, honey?" Sheila asked sleepily. But he didn't need to say a word. His expression said it all. Horror and sorrow.

"Fr..." is all Trent could manage before Captain Pullman resumed his report.

"Anyway, I thought you'd want to know sooner rather than later. His wife found him late yesterday afternoon in the basement. She had asked him to take the trash and when she went to see if he had taken care of it, she found him."

"Please, Captain," Holloway said. "No more. I can't listen to this anymore."

"I understand, Detective. But in light of the fact that Darla and Frank..."

Holloway hung up on his boss.

Trent slowly turned his head towards his wife like a man possessed. "Sheila, Fr... Frank's de...dea...dead," was all he could manage to say before he collapsed on the bed.

A week later, Detective Frank Lion was in the ground next to Jeremy Harris.

The morning was cold and rainy, but Trent went to the cemetery anyway. Soaked to the bone, he paid his respects to his dead colleagues and stood at their gravestones for a long while. He left feeling empty and sad.

Inside his unmarked police car, he brushed his wet

hair from his forehead and wiped his hands on his trousers. He reached into the glove compartment for his pack of cigarettes, shook one out and lit it.

"Those things'll kill you, you know," a voice said from the back seat.

Holloway quickly pulled his police issue nine millimeter from his holster, spun around and aimed.

The face of Pastor William Kline was in his crosshairs.

"DAMMIT!" Holloway yelled. "What the hell are you doing, William?"

"That's funny," Pastor Kline said as he leaned forward, "I was asking myself the same question about you. I figured I'd let you pay your respects before asking. Mind lowering the gun?"

Holloway looked at William then at his pistol. He lowered the gun and dropped it on the passenger seat.

"Thank you. I'm sorry I startled you," Kline apologized.

"That's alright. I like shitting my pants," Holloway said and took a long pull off his cigarette.

Pastor Kline didn't respond to Trent's joke. Instead, he looked at the soggy graveyard and said solemnly, "I think I know what's going on here."

"And what would that be because I haven't got a clue."

"Well, it's going to be difficult for you to believe. In fact, I don't expect you to," Kline said cryptically.

"Oh, I don't know, William. I think I've seen just about everything. Four unsolved homicides of newly pregnant women perpetrated by dead people. A very public suicide. A frozen corpse. One colleague drove straight into a truck and another... well, lets just say he couldn't deal with it anymore and took the easy way out."

174

"The easy way?" Kline said leaning forward, "You think slicing your wrists is easy? Trent, what I'm about to tell you is nothing but horrific."

"So," Holloway insisted, "please tell."

"I don't think we're dealing with a... human being, Trent," Kline hesitated.

"Please tell me, William. I think I deserve to know what you're thinking," Trent said.

"Have you ever read Leviticus in the Bible, or any of the Bishon books?" the pastor asked.

"I've heard of them but never read them," Trent replied.

"Well," Kline started, "In one book, there is a tale of a man who was once a farmer. He was chosen from all the other farmers as Asops, the protector of the land. With his wife, he assumed his duties. In due course, she became pregnant with Asops' son. His life would have been complete but then he lost her."

"Who? His wife? What happened?" Trent asked.

"Yes. His wife. Asops claimed to have lost her as they tried to make their way home during a terrible sand-storm. He was inconsolable, suicidal and eventually lost his mind. Anyway, shortly after his wife disappeared, pregnant women in his village began to show up dead. Beside each body that was discovered, the symbol of the pentagram, a red star, was found."

"Go on," Holloway said with interest.

"As the story goes, the other farmers in the village gathered together and prayed to God to stop the mur-ders. Their prayers went unanswered or so they thought at the time. Not too long after their meeting, vicious weather swept in and wiped out the village." Kline paused to gather his thoughts before resuming the tale. "Months later, as described by Parseps, there was an unwritten law that no woman could be pregnant upon the land, that it was damned for all creation. The land was marked a forbidden place, one that not even God himself could walk upon."

Holloway stared at the pastor.

"The story goes that Asops looked for his son, the son who would have been born if his wife hadn't been lost. He traveled the land and would grab women he met on his search. He would talk to their wombs. And when he did not find his son, he would kill the women," Pastor Kline paused.

Trent cracked open the car window and watched as the smoke escaped into the fresh air.

"Asops was a man desperately in need of love. He was mad with sorrow and had grown weary of the death that surrounded him. As he ventured further and further from his homeland, an outcast and alone, Asops spoke to God, begged him for a sign that would ease his wounded soul. He prayed to Mary Magdalene because in his torment, he had come to believe that she was somehow responsible for what had happened to him. He could not blame himself and did not take responsibility for the deaths he had caused."

"Why was that?" Asked Holloway.

"Well," Kline began, "Asops knew that he would not go unpunished for what he had been doing. He tried to convince himself that his anger drove him to murder innocent women. He made up a story that his wife had died during a miscarriage. He talked to himself constantly and began to believe that his shadow could speak back to him. Asops often had long conversations with his shadow, claiming that it was some sort of holy ghost so that he would escape detection as the insane monster he had become."

Holloway grimaced.

"When Asops reached the mountains," Kline continued, "he met a small farm boy. As the boy approached, Asops' shadow left, explaining that it could not be near the boy."

"Who was the shadow?" Holloway asked.

Kline looked earnestly at the detective. "I don't have to say his name, do I?"

Trent pondered the pastor's question in silence.

William continued. "The small boy was God. That's right. God, disguised as a toddler. When the boy stopped at Asops' feet, Asops knew that the shadow was terrified and had to flee. You see, the shadow had convinced Asops that even though his wife had died, his son did not and had in fact gone to another woman to become a child. The thought drove Asops crazy. The boy explained to Asops that his shadow was evil and that every man has a shadow but what is in it is up to the man. Afterwards, the child disappeared into a cloud of dust and whirling ashes, and Asops' shadow returned in a rage. For his part, Asops was mortified. He felt again the blood on his hands from all the women he had murdered and realized that his actions were based on the Devil's lie. The Devil didn't care about Asops of his son. He wanted to tag along to find a child of his own."

Pastor Kline sat back in his seat and folded his arms across his chest. "If the story is true, and I believe it is, then this evil started a long time ago and has done nothing but grown stronger over the years."

Holloway didn't respond for a long while. Finally, with a great sigh, he looked into his friend's eyes

"William, you're telling me that the guy I'm looking for is from a story in the Bible and that he's still pissed off thousands of years later? That he's some sort of devil worshiper? How am I supposed to believe that? How is it possible that a character from an ancient story has come to life here, now!?" Holloway slicked back his damp hair and lit another cigarette.

"Trent," Pastor Kline said in all seriousness. "The man you're looking for not a devil worshiper. He is the Antichrist."

Trent Holloway felt goose flesh rise on his arms. He turned from the pastor and took a drag off his cigarette.

"William," Trent began gently, "How would it be possible? Do you really believe that you can convince me that the Antichrist is alive and well and living in Shallow Front?"

"Yes, Trent. I do believe it's possible. After all, we believe that God is here, don't we?" Pastor Kline asked.

Trent tentatively replied, "Yes, we do, William."

"So wouldn't it be possible for the Antichrist to be here as well?" Kline asked rhetorically.

"I guess it is possible," Trent conceded. "But if the Antichrist is walking the earth in the form of a man..."

"That would explain everything, wouldn't it, Trent?"

Trent thought it over. "The sulfur smell at the crime

scenes... hell fire. Billy Warrington cutting his own throat... the devil made him do it..."

Pastor Kline's eyes lit up, "Yes, my boy. And lest we not forget that the killer favors only pregnant women. Ask yourself, why is that?"

Both men looked at each other with wide eyes.

"We've been having dreams. I'm sure some of the victims had dreams. All the same dreams, too. You've had them. You're just too afraid to admit it," Pastor Kline challenged.

Trent Holloway's composure snapped then. "William, get out of the car. Now. I don't want to hear anymore of this horseshit. I don't believe it."

William opened the back door and stepped into the rain. "Think about it, Trent! You think about what I said!! Think about God!!"

Trent Holloway sped away, leaving Pastor Kline alone in the cemetery.

As he drove the side streets of Shallow Front, Holloway thought about Frank Lion. He didn't know why Frank slashed his wrists. He thought about Jeremy's accident in spite of his excellent driving skills. He thought about Bill Warrington's outrageous action, and he thought about his own dreams. Trent did not want to believe Pastor Kline. He didn't. But what other explanation was there? He had to consider the possibility that what Pastor Kline said might be true.

Then Holloway remembered the note found on Darla Goodman's body and began to believe that Kline might be right. But he hoped he was wrong. The very thought made Detective Holloway want to scream.

The way Frank looked at the victim. Like he knew her.

"I don't know," Holloway said out loud trying to convince himself that it was not possible. But Pastor Kline was right about the dreams.

He was right about the dreams.

As Holloway drove back to the station house, he started to formulate a plan. He was determined to catch John Doe. There would be no next time for their serial killer.

But Trent was wrong.

Heather Mills waited at the counter at the Won Ton restaurant around the corner from Gussby's for her take-out lunch. She wasn't thinking about much more than eating and staying dry. It was raining again.

The smell of fried dumplings and sesame chicken made her stomach growl. At the same time, the little bell above the door jingled. Another customer entered the Chinese restaurant.

"Damn, it sure is pouring out there," he said as he shook the rain off his clothing. His eyes connected with Heather's, and he smiled.

But Heather wasn't interested in the smile. She had become disillusioned with men ever since she found out that her boyfriend was cheating on her. Apparently, he was more into brunettes than blondes, and you didn't get much more blonde than Heather Mills.

"Excuse me, ma'am. Do you know where I can get some wine?" the man asked.

Heather turned. "I don't know, chief. I don't drink." She glanced at her ticket and was happy to see that there were only three more numbers before hers was called. She didn't want to make small talk with the man, especially in light of what was going on in Shallow Front.

"Thank you, anyway," he said.

Heather glanced at him as he turned to leave. He was not at all unattractive. He wore a black leather jacket and his hair was slicked back with gel. His brown eyes were deep-set and he had a really great smile.

"You know," Heather spun around, "come to think of it, there is a place down the road about five blocks from here. It's called the Orchid, and I think they have a pretty good selection."

The man's eyes were pleasant. Heather couldn't help but be drawn in.

"I appreciate it," he said and winked at her. He opened the door to leave just as Heather grabbed her food. He held it for her, and she thanked him.

When she reached her car, she opened the passenger side door first and placed her lunch on the seat. As she shut the door, she saw that her tire was flat. A nail was sticking out of the sidewall.

"Shit!" she cursed. It was raining harder. "Shit, shit, shit!!" she screamed. "Where's a damn cop when you need one?"

Heather got the jack and the lug wrench out of the trunk and bent down to change the tire.

"Shit!" she said again in frustration as she attempted to loosen the lug nuts off the rim. They wouldn't budge.

"Need some help?" a voice asked from behind her.

Heather spun around. It was him. "Yes," she said with a coy smile, "I most definitely do. Thanks."

The man took the wrench from Heather. She stood to the side and watched as he turned the lug nuts with ease and replaced her flat tire with the doughnut she had in her trunk.

"Now why couldn't I do that?" Heather asked with a giggle.

"Well, sometimes it takes a little ummmmph, you know?" he replied with a flirtatious smile. "You know, you're going to have to get a new tire. It's not safe to drive around on the doughnut for too long."

"Well, I will. Thank you. And thank you for helping me." Heather liked his manners and the lock of hair that fell on his forehead.

"No problem, ma'am," the man said as he began to walk away.

"Hey!" Heather yelled, "Need a lift?"

The man turned towards her. *God he's gorgeous,* she thought.

"Sure wouldn't mind one. Thanks." He hurried back to her car and jumped in the passenger seat.

"Mind if I smoke?" she asked.

"Absolutely not. It's your car, ma'am."

"I feel so silly but I didn't ask you your name."

The man held out his hand, "It's Harold."

Shaking his hand unnerved Heather. He was superbly strong and smelled so good. She noticed that his leather jacket was beautifully tailored and that he wore cowboy boots with chrome tips. A soothing, warm feeling crawled up her neck. In fact, she was beginning to feel warm somewhere else as well.

"Aren't you going to tell me yours?" he asked.

"What?" Heather asked. "Oh, oh. My name. My name is Heather." His nearness distracted her. "Do you live around here, Harold?"

"Yep, East Side Garrison City. I live near New York, actually. Do you know where East Side is?"

"Sure do," she said. "My ex-boyfriend lives out that way."

"Ex?" Harold asked.

"Yes, ex. He's an asshole."

"Sorry. I didn't mean to pry," Harold seemed embarrassed.

"No problem. Really," Heather said. "I'm over him."

They parked across from the wine shop. The rain had begun to fall again.

"I kinda lied," Heather confessed. "I do drink wine. I just didn't know if I could trust you because of what's been going on lately, you know?"

"I do, and I don't blame you. I'm kinda looking over my shoulder, too," Harold said.

"But why? Are you pregnant?" Heather laughed.

"Well, no, but I...I'm..." Harold stammered.

"I'm just kidding," Heather said as she poked him in the shoulder.

"Well, it's good to see someone in this town still has a sense of humor," Harold said.

Heather looked into Harold's eyes and smiled. Her mind was swirling. She didn't know what was happening, but she liked it.

"I kinda lied, too," Harold admitted. His voice was

deep, rugged and sexy.

"What was that?" Heather asked, her Chinese food long forgotten.

"I came here to buy the wine for you. When I saw you at WonTon's, I thought you were the most beautiful woman I had ever seen, and I came up with the wine excuse just to talk to you." Harold blushed.

"You're kidding, right?"

"Yes," he said, then gave her a goofy look. She burst out laughing. "Anyway, thanks for the ride, Heather," he smiled.

Heather jumped a little in her seat when she heard her name spoken with that sexy voice.

"Hey, Harold. What are you doing later tonight?" she boldly asked.

"I don't have any plans. Why?"

"Oh, just wondering. Well if you're not busy, why don't you meet me at Gussby's Tavern? Maybe we could sit and talk for a while."

"I'd like that," Harold smiled.

"Great!" Heather was giddy. "Meet me there about seven?"

"OK, I will. Stay dry," Harold said as he reached for her hand and grasped it. "See you later."

She watched as the sexy stranger went into the Orchid. His touch made her heart leap a little. She liked it.

Trent prepared the conference room by taping a map of Shallow Front and the surrounding towns to the chalkboard. He stood in front of it as a dozen patrolmen settled into their seats. Captain Pullman was in attendance as were another half dozen special agents. Simon Fielding who led the raid on Willie Zigs leaned against the far wall, his arms folded across his chest.

Detective Holloway began, "As you all know, four women have been brutally murdered in the last six months in these four areas." Holloway pointed to the red circles on the map. "The methods by which they were murdered are not similar, but I believe that the motive for each killing is consistent."

"What do you want us to do?" Officer David Squall asked. "Our hands are tied."

"Well, I have prepared a report for all of you detailing each homicide. May I remind you that the information in these packets is confidential and must not be discussed with anyone other than those attending this meeting," Holloway warned. "In addition to the crime scene and autopsy reports, we have had the F.B.I. profilers develop a profile of our John Doe. Basically, we are looking for a white male, highly intelligent, stealthy which could mean agile, age 35 to 50. Physically, we believe that he is quite strong, tall and thin, six feet to six feet four, 175 - 200 pounds. He likes to wear expensive clothing."

"What about a cowboy hat?" one of the officers asked.

Trent's jaw dropped. "What makes you ask that question, Officer?"

"I've been having these weird dreams, sir. I wake up remembering a man sort of like the one you've described wearing a black cowboy hat."

"You, too?" another officer chimed in.

"Yes," the first cop replied. "Nightmares, really. Practically every night."

"I never see his face, though. The hat covers his eyes," yet another officer added.

Holloway felt icy fear slip down his spine.

"In my dreams, the man is walking a wolf like you would walk a dog," Private Benson said as he looked up at Detective Holloway.

The conference room grew very quiet.

Trent had to say something. "Look, people. These dreams you've been having, they're just weird coincidences. That's all."

"You really believe that, Detective?" Officer Milson asked.

Trent cleared his throat and looked sternly at the young man. "I don't know what to believe. But I do know one thing for sure. There is an explanation for everything. There always is, and it's our job to find it. So pay attention out there and if something doesn't feel right, investigate it. No matter how trivial. We are going to catch this guy!"

And with that, the officers and agents collected their reports and filed out of the conference room.

Heather Mills met her new friend at Gussby's at 7pm as he promised. She was a little nervous that he would stand her up. But he didn't, and she was so relieved. A guy like Harold doesn't come along every day.

Harold ordered a draught beer and swirled the golden liquid around in his glass. Next to him, Heather smoked a cigarette and moved her head back and forth to the jukebox music.

"You like country?" she asked.

"Well..." he started, "Actually, I prefer rock and roll."

"Oh," Heather said and changed the subject. "Where are you from? And how old are you, anyway? I can't tell."

Harold laughed. "Well, I'm old enough to know better than to answer that question. As for where I'm from? Well, I was born in Virginia, but I've lived all over the country." He sipped his beer and asked, "Wh-what about you?"

"Me?" Heather's eyes widened. "I grew up upstate New York."

Harold signaled for another beer.

"Here you go, pal," Gussby said as he placed another cold beer on the bar.

"What do you do? I never asked you that either," Heather said as her favorite song began to play.

"I'm a construction worker," Harold replied. "I guess you could say I build things, all kinds of things."

"Really?" Heather commented. "My apartment needs all kinds of work."

Heather grabbed Harold by his sleeve. He smelled of soap and musk. She loved being close to him.

"Please," Heather said taking Harold's hand, "dance with me."

"Sure," he replied.

They danced to a slow country tune. Harold's chin rested on Heather's shoulder. His hand fit perfectly in the small of her back. She rested her head against his solid and warm chest.

There was no escape now for Heather. She was a prisoner to his eyes and her infatuation. Lust exploded in her mind and in her body. Harold smelled good, looked good and knew all the right things to say. And he could dance. Part of Heather wanted to run but most of the rest of her wanted to take him home with her right away.

As they swayed together on the dance floor, Trent Holloway walked into Gussby.

Well, well. Look at Heather, he thought.

Trent went to the bar and ordered a beer. It had been another frustrating day for him, and the revelation at the morning meeting had disturbed him more than he would admit. A beer was just the thing to take the edge off.

Heather and her date swayed slowly on the dance floor. She seemed happy and that made Trent feel better. Ever since Jeremy died, she hadn't been the same. Trent didn't know for sure but he guessed that Jeremy and his secretary had once dated.

On the dance floor, Heather was in her glory. "Oh Harold," she cooed. "If only I had met you before. I would have saved myself so much trouble."

"Heather, would you like to go out again?" he asked.

Heather looked at him sweetly and said, "I'd like that."

The song ended, and Harold led her back to her stool at the bar. She was surprised to see that Trent Holloway had taken a seat next to hers.

"Hello, Detective," Heather said cheerfully.

"Hey, Heather. How's my favorite secretary?" Trent casually asked.

"Not bad. This is my friend, Harold, uhh, what's your last name?" Heather asked.

"Miller."

Holloway extended his hand.

"Nice to meet you," Harold said as he shook it.

"Same here, Harold. Would you excuse Heather a moment. I need to talk to her outside."

"What about?" Heather asked, frowning.

"Please, Heather. Captain Pullman wanted me to find you to tell you something. It'll be brief," Trent said.

Heather looked at Harold who was nursing his beer. He nodded as if she had his approval. Oh how Heather wanted to kiss his face. He was godlike, shimmering with a tan that accentuated his perfect white teeth. Heather wondered how he kept them so clean and perfect.

"See you in a minute," she sighed.

"Sure," Harold said and smiled sadly, "Sure you're coming back?"

"You can bet on it!" Heather said.

Once outside with Trent Holloway, Heather's mood changed completely. "This better be good, Detective Holloway," she spat at him.

Trent took his time lighting his cigarette, infuriating Heather even more. "Want one?" he offered. Heather shook her head no.

"You sure?" Holloway asked.

"Of course I'm sure. What did you want to talk about?" Heather asked impatiently.

"Captain Pullman wanted you to be the beneficiary of Jeremy's life insurance policy instead of the precinct." Trent didn't expect the reaction he got.

Heather started to cry. "I can't believe he would want to give your share to me."

"Well, he knows you've been having a rough time without Jeremy and since he had no family..." Trent didn't need to continue. Heather cried harder.

"Hey, Heather. Don't cry. You can't go back in there with a red face," Trent said, appealing to her vanity.

Heather gingerly patted her cheeks and eyes to avoid messing up her make-up. "You're right, Trent. It's just that I'm so...happy."

"Well, I can see that. Who's your friend? I haven't seen you smile like that in weeks."

"I met him just today. He changed my flat tire."

"Well, I sure am glad to hear that chivalry is not dead," Trent said with a smile and glanced up at Harold Miller through Gussby's big plate glass window. "He sure does seem like a..." Detective Holloway stopped short. *What the...?*

"Trent. Trent, what's wrong?" Heather asked.

It can't be, Holloway thought. He closed his eyes and shook his head. When he looked again, Harold Miller was sitting just where they left him. *It can't be.*

"Trent, are you OK?" Heather asked.

Holloway didn't answer. He was too lost in thought. When he glanced at Heather's date the first time through the window, he thought he saw someone else instead, an old man with straggly gray hair wearing a moth eaten suit. A second later, well-dressed Harold Miller was there instead. Had his eyes played a trick on him?

"Heather. Oh. Nothing's wrong. Sorry," Trent apologized.

"Well, I'll be getting back to my date now," Heather said. "And thank you for the news about the life insurance policy. I'll thank Captain Pullman myself tomorrow." And with a little wave and a big smile, Heather skipped back into Gussby's.

Something's wrong. Trent watched through the window as Heather and Harold flirted and laughed with each other. But for the life of him, he couldn't say what was bothering him. A memory was on the tip of his brain, but somehow, it had evaporated like a puff of smoke. Then he remembered. He had forgotten his umbrella at the office. Trent got back into his car and looked at Heather again. She seemed so happy.

It was the last time he saw her alive.

Trent Holloway realized that he hadn't paid for the beer he hadn't finished and returned to Gussby's to do both.

When he entered, he noticed that Heather was gone.

Trent resumed his seat at the bar and motioned for Gus to come over.

"Hey, Gus. Think you can get me a fresh one?" he asked as he put a ten on the bar.

"Sure, Detective Holloway," Gussby replied. He grabbed a cold beer out of the fridge and handed it to Trent.

"I sure am glad you went and had a talk with Heather. Something's come over that girl, and I'll be damned if that scene tonight wasn't one of the strangest things I seen in a while."

Trent sipped his beer and asked, "What are you talking about, Gus?"

"What am I talking about? You seen him, Detective. That guy Heather brought in here," Gussby shook his head in disgust and continued. "He looked like he fell down a sewer and climbed out. I sure was worried about her. But then you had a chat with her outside there and she left not a minute later."

"Gus, I gotta tell you, I don't know what you're talking about. Harold, Heather's date, looked real clean-cut to me. A nice guy," Trent said truly perplexed.

Guss grabbed his forehead and roughly pushed back the few hairs on his bald head. "You mean to tell me that you couldn't smell that guy?"

Holloway looked deeply into Gus' eyes and realized that he wasn't kidding. "Gus, indulge me. Tell me exactly what you saw."

Gussby sighed and looked at Trent like he was crazy but told him anyway. "Harold, or whatever his name is, was about 60. I guess he was about 5-9, 5-10, scrawny like he hadn't eaten a good meal in a while. His jacket was an old brown plaid number with moth holes all over it. He wore it over a stained blue shirt and red tie. If the guy had three teeth, it were a lot. The couple I saw were brown."

All of what Gus told him was startling but eerily, vaguely familiar. Then Trent remembered.

"Gus," Trent grabbed the bar owner by the arm. "This is important. Did you see Harold get into the car with Heather?"

"Trent, hey, you're hurting me, pal."

Holloway eased up and apologized.

"I told you already. Heather left first, like a minute after your little chat. Mr. Wonderful left probably another minute after that."

Trent knew Heather. And he knew that there was no way she would let Harold, her Harold, out of her grasp.

Heather Mills didn't take Harold home with her. She took him to the Arliss Hotel instead.

The drive on the winding roads out of town and past Lincoln took almost forty minutes. But that was OK. It gave Heather time to think. Should she have sex with him or not? It could end up just another one night stand and be completely meaningless. Or...

Every so often, she looked over at Harold and smiled. She could probably get used to calling him her boyfriend.

Harold smelled of fresh cut wood and cinnamon with a touch of lemon. And he was so handsome. There was no way she would let another woman grab her prize. And that's definitely what he was, a prize. Heather wanted him all to herself.

"You've been pretty quiet," Harold said as the glow from the dashboard lights illuminated his dark eyes.

"I'm just thinking. That's all," Heather replied.

A minute later, they pulled into the Arliss Motel's parking lot. Heather opened the car windows and killed the engine. They each smoked a cigarette and looked at the motel's entrance. Heather made up both their minds.

"Come with me, Harold," she said as she took his hand.

At nine-thirty that evening, the same maid who waited on the Holloways, Sister, was vacuuming the lobby carpets. The night clerk was reading a horror novel.

Sister shut off the vacuum and said to Benny, "How can you read those damn things, child? They give me nightmares."

"I don't know, Sister," Benny said, "I guess I just grew up on'em."

"Well," Sister replied, "I would throw up on them! My stomach's too weak for those scary stories." The phone rang just then and interrupted their conversation. Benny answered it.

"Arliss front desk. Benny speaking. How may I help you?"

"Yes, Benny. This is Mark Robins in room two-thirteen. I have a complaint about the people next door in two-fourteen. They've been blaring opera music for the past hour and it's late. I have to get some sleep."

"I'm on my way, sir. I apologize for any inconvenience," Benny said.

"Hey, Sister, do me a favor?" Benny asked. "Please go to two-fourteen and ask those nice people to turn down their music? You remember them?"

"Sure do," Sister said. "The pretty little blonde and her looker."

"Yep, that's them. Please take care of it."

Sister rested the vacuum against the wall and walked up the stairs to the second floor. She cursed all the way. *Why in the hell can't Benny do this? Why do I always have to be the pain in the ass? So what if their music's a little loud? Better than running up and down the halls naked with their fingers in their asses!*

Sister didn't need to know the room number to determine where the music was coming from. Some lady was singing her heart out behind door two-fourteen. Sister clearly understood why Mr. Robbins was upset. The volume was up so high, the floors vibrated.

It didn't help at all that the door was ajar and the music leaked out into the hallway. Sister knocked on the door and it started to swing open.

"Hello?" she yelled over the music. "I don't want to just barge in here but I have to do something about the music."

Sister noticed the Do Not Disturb sign hung on the outside of the door. *Why leave the door open with that sign on there?* she wondered. *Are they smoking dope or something?*

"Fuck it," Sister mumbled and pushed the door all the way open. What she saw when she looked inside made her jaw drop.

The handsome man and the pretty blonde were dancing. His eyes twinkled as he guided her around the room with one arm around her back and the other holding hers out to the side. The girl was so beautiful. But her feet were not touching the floor.

They were three feet off the ground.

Sister couldn't help it. Her eyes drifted upward and she saw that a length of rope had been tied to the heavy old ceiling fan. She followed the rope down and saw that it ended in a loop around the girl's neck. The girl was swaying back and forth to the rhythm of the ceiling fan's blades.

And an old man was dancing with her now.

Sister screamed.

"Do you mind?" Harold Miller asked.

Sister stopped screaming.

"The sign says do not disturb," the Antichrist said in a voice so evil that Sister knew it was not human.

Harold Miller stepped closer to Sister. His shimmering black eyes held her captive. His breath wreaked of death.

"Of course," Harold said as he held the straight razor from Frank Lion's basement up to her face. "Anyone can cut in if they want."

Sister backed out of the room and ran for her life.

Trent Holloway had just left Heather's apartment building when he got the call.

As soon as he left Gussby's, he put out an APB on Heather Mills. Holloway sensed that she was in great danger and wanted her to be located before it was too late.

It was too late.

Trent made the trip to the Arliss in less than 20 minutes, flying over the winding roads with a recklessness he didn't know he possessed. *How could I have let the creep slip through my fingers?* he shouted at himself. *I killed her.*

The medical examiner's van had just pulled into the parking lot ahead of him. Captain Pullman was already waiting in the motel's lobby. Two police officers were interviewing a very agitated middle-aged black woman, and Officer Squall was questioning the front desk clerk.

Holloway approached the woman. "Officers, I'll take it from here. But stay close. You'll need to take her downtown after I talk to her," Holloway said.

"Yes, sir."

Holloway looked at Sister. Her lips trembled and mascara-black tears streaked her face.

"I know you're upset, but I need you to talk to me," Holloway said softly.

"Um, OK, Detective," Sister muttered.

"Tell me what you saw."

Sister held her breath a moment before telling her story.

"It all happened so fast, but I'll never forget what I saw. Ever," she began. She lifted her eyes to Trent's and didn't look away. It was if she expected an answer to the insanity she witnessed.

"The door was open a bit, and the music was so loud, I could hardly hear myself call out to them. I knew they sure as hell couldn't hear me. So I pushed the door open and there they was. Dancing. Except that pretty young thing was hanging in the air, and that handsome young man was twirling her around like they was on a big dance floor. He spun her around and around. One second he was young and then when he came out from behind her, he was old. Disgusting. Filthy clothes. Filthy hair. He didn't have but a few teeth. And then that young man showed up again. I thought I was seeing things, you know, making it all up in my head." Sister paused and gulped some air. Her body quivered when she exhaled.

"I knew it was real though when I looked at that girl's face. Her eyes was open, looking at nothing like they was looking at something. The whites weren't white any more. They were red. And her neck and face were blue. The rope creaked under her weight. That's when I snapped to. That old man was back, and he was laughing like he was having a grand old time. He was staring real hard at me. Then he pulled out a straight razor, and I ran like hell down here and called the police from that phone right over there." Sister pointed to the front desk.

"You need a drink of water or anything?" Trent asked.

"No, sir. I just need to get the hell out of here," she replied.

"In a minute, Sister." Trent was kind but firm. "Did you see anyone leave?"

"I didn't. I heard the motherfucker laughing as I ran away. I thought he was gonna come after me. So I grabbed Benny, and we ran outside to my car. I keep a thirty-eight in the glove box so I got it.

"Where's it now?" Holloway asked.

"The police took it from me," she replied. "Anyway, me and Benny heard the fire alarm ring. The guy must have opened the window because he set off the alarm."

"You didn't see him again?" Trent asked

"No, I didn't. And I never want to. But I know I will every night in my dreams." Sister started to shake and cry again.

"Sister, you're going to have to go down to the station tonight to fill out a report and talk to a sketch artist. You think you're up for that?"

"I'll try, Detective," she said weakly.

"Good," Holloway said and smiled at her warmly. He motioned to the two officers to come and get Sister and watched as they wrapped a blanket around her and ushered into the patrol car.

"Officer Squall," Holloway asked. "What did Benny have to say?"

"Well, he said that the man who came in with the victim was a broad shouldered, white male, approximately six foot three, a hundred and eighty pounds. He said he had dark eyes, was very tan and clean shaven with black hair. As a matter of fact, Benny said his hair was so black it almost looked blue."

"Okay," Holloway shrugged, "What else?"

"Well," David Squall said, "He was wearing a black jacket and was very polite."

Holloway couldn't breath. He was now sure that it was the same man from Gussby's. He finally knew who the killer was. *Or do I?*

"Detective, are you alright?" Squall asked.

"Yeah," he replied with a faraway look in his eyes. "Yeah, David, I'm fine. Listen, I need to go outside for a minute, gather my thoughts. If you see Pullman, tell him I'll be right back," Trent said.

Detective Holloway walked out the front doors of The Arliss Hotel and stared into the night. Snow was falling heavily again. A cold breeze caressed his face and he shuddered.

Could it be? he thought. *Could Heather have been pregnant?*

If what Pastor Kline had told him was true, then yes, Heather was pregnant and didn't yet know it.

"No," he heard himself say. *How could he have known it if she didn't even know it?*

Chapter 12

When the story of yet another murder broke on Channel 6 News the next day, Mary Showalter was in her kitchen making herself a peanut butter and jelly sandwich for dinner. The news report interrupted her favorite sitcom.

"Good Lord," Mary said to Rex, her ferocious-looking but very gentle Doberman Pinscher. Posted on the screen were sketches of two suspects, one, a disturbingly ugly old man, and the other, a handsome younger man with jet black hair. The younger man reminded Mary of the way her husband, Mark, used to look.

Mark reluctantly left town on a business trip. He did not want to leave his pregnant wife home alone, but the trip would mean both a raise and a promotion and God knew he needed both with a baby on the way. The weekend before he left, he bought Mary a handgun and taught her how to shoot it. With Rex to stand guard and the gun in case Rex was not successful, Mark felt better about leaving his wife alone.

It was a very cold winter's night, but Mary felt warm and cozy in her home. Rex crunched on a Milkbone as Mary settled into her easy chair, her sandwich and a glass of milk already waiting for her on the coffee table.

She curled her knees up under her, covered them with a blanket and ate her sandwich while watching the television. The news report was gone from her mind and in its place was her sitcom. She laughed out loud as the strong wind rattled the windows and doors.

This time, he waited breathing normally. This time would be his last time in Shallow Front. If he couldn't find what he was looking for here, he would move on to someplace else, and that was just fine. He was beginning to feel uneasy. The cop. The one who saw Harold Miller through the window at the bar. It was if he wasn't looking at him but right through him.

The Antichrist stepped into Mary Showalter's bathroom carrying an axe by his side and closed the door. He would make the room his own until she came in.

He waits.

Trent Holloway called on Pastor William Kline the morning after the murder.

"Morning, William," Trent said as the Pastor invited him into the kitchen, "I figured it was time to come on by and help you with that stump out back."

"Let me get my coat. I'll just be a minute," Pastor Kline said.

He returned wearing his down jacket with the hood up, a wool scarf and heavy fleece gloves. "Ready when you are!"

They grabbed shovels from the shed and started to clear away the fresh snow from the stump.

"Trent, I don't think you came over here just to help me with this stump," Kline surmised. "Tell me, son, what are you going to do?"

Trent wasn't the least bit surprised that Pastor Kline could see right through him. "William," he began, "I really don't know."

Trent lowered his eyes and stared at the hard ground. His heart ached, especially when he thought of Heather. He could have prevented her death.

Why did he look like an old man?

"William, I don't understand why this is happening. Here. Now. Why, William?" Holloway asked with tears in his eyes.

"All I can say to you, Trent, is that you are dealing with something extraordinary."

Trent looked at Pastor Kline skeptically. "And what if I am beginning to believe you, William. What then?"

"Then I suggest you pray," William answered.

Trent took the pointed shovel from Pastor Kline's hand. "Let me have a try at this stump."

"Be my guest. Moving it is harder than it looks," William said.

Trent attacked the base of the stump with the tip of the shovel. "I'm never gonna catch this guy, am I?"

"Trent, you do what you know how to do, but I'll tell you something you probably already understand. These deaths are different. The man you seek is cunning and has but one goal."

"To murder all the pregnant women in Shallow Front,"

Trent concluded.

"No, I don't agree," Pastor Kline said as he shook his head. "I think he is inclined to murder every pregnant women in the world until he finds what he is looking for."

"And what exactly is he looking for, William?"

"He is looking for his lost son," William replied.

Trent looked at his friend with resignation. "Okay. Suppose what you say is true, and the story about Asops is true. What does it all have to do with Shallow Front?"

"Trent," Kline began, "if we are indeed dealing with the devil, the Antichrist, he works in the same mysterious ways as the Lord."

Trent stopped prying at the roots of the stump and pulled a pack of cigarettes from his flannel shirt pocket.

"Think about it, Detective. Even though you are a believer in faith and in good Christian righteousness, you are also a non-believer in Satan," Kline said.

Holloway smiled weakly and blew out a stream of smoke. "William, excuse me for saying so, but I..."

The pastor interrupted, "You are a cop. You believe what you see with your own eyes. But the truth is, in this situation, you are blind. You can't accept the fact that true evil is walking the earth. I truly believe that this man *is* the Antichrist."

Holloway grimaced. Could it truly be that the Devil is watching, waiting and murdering pregnant women?

"Think, Trent," Pastor Kline implored. "Think about Jeremy Harris and Frank Lion."

"Why? What about them?" Trent asked.

"You don't really believe that the deaths of Harris and Lion were coincidences, do you?"

"Jeremy was in the wrong place at the wrong time and..."

"A story that you keep telling yourself, Trent," Kline interjected.

"...and Detective Lion was upset by Darla Goodman's murder," Trent finished.

Pastor Kline shook his head. "Let me assure you that Frank Lion had no faith in God. If he had, he wouldn't have committed the sin of suicide. He was coerced, persuaded into slicing his wrists. Any sane man, no matter how distraught, would not have done what he did. He had a family, Trent."

"You know, William. I think you're crazy. I think you're a crazy old man."

"I don't think you believe that, Trent. You are simply resisting the obvious truth," William said gently. "Didn't the note bother you? Haven't all of them? And what you told me about seeing an old man for that split second instead of Heather's handsome, young date. Why do you think that happened, Trent? Is it because you have no faith? Or is it because you do? Perhaps God allowed you to see evil because He is trying to help you."

"William, I'm having a difficult time dealing with these theories of yours," Trent said. "I'd really rather not talk about them anymore."

"I am only telling you the truth, Detective. Nothing more," Pastor Kline said with a passion Trent Holloway couldn't ignore.

Who will paint for me? the first note had said, *down in hell...*

Mary Showalter stretched like a cat under the blanket and rubbed her belly. It was time to take a bath and go to sleep.

Rex took a break from the bone he was working on and looked up at his owner. The big dog cocked his head to the side as he watched Mary go through her routine of double-checking the locks on all the windows and doors.

"Please," she whispered a prayer to herself, "Please, dear God, don't let that madman come calling on me."

"Why can't we move?" Sheila Holloway asked as she lay next to her husband in their bed. Trent wrapped his arms tightly around his wife.

"Honey, all I need to do is solve this case, arrest this madman, and all will be the same as it was before."

Sheila snuggled in the warmth and closeness of her husband.

"Sheila, he's gonna make a mistake. Sooner or later they always do," Trent said with a confidence he didn't quite feel.

Do I have faith? Trent asked himself. *Does it really matter anyway?*

Mary looked at her reflection in the bathroom mirror and felt very alone, more alone than she ever had in her whole life. She missed her husband and her family. They lived so far away, and, with the baby coming and all, she really needed to be near them.

Maybe we'll go visit them this summer, she thought as

she looked at the colorful shower curtain with all the pretty fish. *We could go to the beach.* To Mary, there was no better place to reconcile your thoughts than the beach, with a cold drink in your hand and your toes sifting the soft, warm sand.

Maybe we could move down there, she thought. But Mary knew Mark would never want to go, especially when he returned from his business with a promotion.

"It must be hormones," she said aloud and laughed at herself.

Mary rinsed out the tub and ran a bath with her favorite bubble bath. She watched herself in the mirror as she put her hair up in a loose bun. She didn't notice the eyes spying her through the slats of the closet door. With the reflection from the bathroom light, they came alive and reflected like shiny dimes.

Mary was about to reach into the closet and pull out a towel when she realized that she had left her robe on the couch.

"Shit," she said as she trudged back into the living room. Mary decided to turn on the radio before heading back into the bathroom. After trying a few stations, she found one that played mellow R&B. A Luther song came on, and she sighed.

The bathroom was nice and steamy when she returned, and the bubbles rimmed the edge of the tub. She shut off the water, slipped her nightgown over her head and turned to hang it next to her robe on a hook behind the door. When she turned back around, Harold Miller, the old Harold Miller, stood in front of her.

"Tell me your name," he said as he brought the axe tip

up to her cheek.

Mary couldn't scream or move as she watched the axe come closer and closer to her face. The blackened, pointed fingernails of the filthy man flicked across the sharp edge of the blade. Mary watched as he drooled like a dog anticipating a tasty treat. And then she fainted.

Harold Miller, the Antichrist, effortlessly picked her up off the tile floor and tossed her into the hall outside the bathroom. His mouth watered in luscious delight as he anticipated what he would next do. He had imagined how her blood felt and tasted for hours. And the time was upon him.

In the living room, Rex growled a low, ominous growl. He padded slowly towards the bathroom with his head down and his docked ears on high alert. The Antichrist matched the dog's rumblings in the same murderous way. Harold Miller, who had died many years ago from alcohol poisoning, stood over Mary Showalter's unconscious body and pulled his pants off. With animalistic brutality, he fell on her and raped her as Rex whimpered down the hall.

When Harold was finished raping Mary's now lifeless body, he looked up at Rex and bared his teeth. Hot urine leaked from under the dog and spread in a puddle on the hardwood floor. Harold held out his hand and walked slowly towards the Doberman.

Rex made a wild lurch at the hand. Harold swatted at his muzzle and Rex fell to the floor, whimpering. He made to clean his soiled hindquarters but instead, bit into his own stomach.

Blood stained Rex's canine teeth as he pulled ferociously on his own skin. He ripped open his abdomen blood and intestines poured out. Rex threw his head violently on the floor. His skull cracked with hellish snap and he was dead.

Harold smiled then and stepped over the gruesome remains of the dog. The Antichrist stepped into the living room and tapped a black cigarette out of a silver case. When he lit it, the smoke swirled in the air and transformed itself into ghostly images of Cassandra Evans, Amanda Dawson, Jessica Frommel, Heather Mills and Mary Showalter.

Before leaving, Harold grabbed Mary and his axe and surveyed his handiwork with a satisfaction.

I am the wolf among all the sheep.

Trent Holloway's dream that same evening was the worst one yet.

In his dream, he was driving through the snow. Detton was in the passenger seat, crying because he missed his mommy so much.

"We'll be home soon, kiddo," Trent said.

With no warning, Holloway's police car suddenly slid sideways. He tried to bring it under control but failed. They crashed into a telephone pole.

"Son of a bitch!" Holloway yelled. Detton cried harder.

"You alright, son?" he asked.

"Yes, Daddy. MOMMMMMMMMY!"

Trent opened the door. "Come on, Detton." Once they were out of the car, the smell of antifreeze assaulted their noses.

Holding his son's hand, Holloway walked toward a pay phone at the end of the street.

"MOMMMMMMMY!" Detton wailed.

Suddenly, Trent smelled burning matches.

"MOMMMMMY!!" Detton screamed again.

"Detton, SHUT UP!" Trent scolded.

"Don't you tell him to shut up," a voice from over Trent's right shoulder said.

Trent turned toward the voice. He saw himself hunched over in the snow. He was holding an axe and crying blood just like the porcelain angel on Jeremy Harris' desk.

Trent woke up screaming.

When she stepped inside the grocery store next door to Gussby's the morning after Mary Showalter's assault, Sister wasn't feeling very well. She would have stayed home, but she needed a few ingredients to make her never-fails-cures-everything chicken soup. She thought she was coming down with the flu.

Ever since the murder at the Arliss, Sister hadn't worked. So what little money she had, she spent on food, not a flu shot.

As she checked out, Sister noticed that the clerk wasn't smiling like she used to. No one was smiling for that matter. For the tenth time that morning, Sister thought she had better get out of Shallow Front before everybody forgot even how to smile.

She trudged through the heavy snow back to the warmth of her little apartment. Her big down coat kept her warm in spite of the strong, gusty wind. But Sister found it difficult to keep the grocery bag in her arms. It kept slipping.

She was almost to Carson Park when the bag tore. She lost her eggs and bacon to a snow pile. And a single can of peas escaped and rolled down the hill of a side street. Sister clutched the grocery bag tighter and chased after it as best she could.

The can of peas was behaving strangely, however, more like a feather in the wind than a heavy object. Every time Sister got close to it, it evaded her grasp as if some force was guiding it. At one point, it actually changed direction.

Can the wind make that happen? Sister thought.

Finally, the can rolled to a stop.

Sister bent down and grabbed the can, eager to get out of the cold but dreading the climb back up the hill.

As she turned around, she saw movement out of the corner of her eye. She stood in front of a chain link fence that blocked an alley. Sister approached the fence and peered through it.

In front of her, about a hundred feet away, were several condemned apartment buildings. Sister knew they had been abandoned a long time but that the city just never got around to tearing them down.

She scanned the doorways of the buildings until she spotted the source of the movement that brought her there in the first place. In an instant, her hand flew up to her mouth to stifle her scream. It was him. The man from the Arliss. He was walking up the stairs of one of the old apartment buildings.

Sister saw that he was wearing a suit and that he was carrying something, but she couldn't make out what it was. She did, however, see him pause and raise his head as if he heard something.

As it turned out, that something was the beating heart of a frightened black woman holding a grocery bag against her chest.

Sister ran. She dropped her groceries and pulled herself up the hill towards Center Square and Main Street.

Show me the way Lord, she thought. And he did. He gave her a payphone.

With the new evidence in hand, Trent Holloway met with six U.S. Marshals and several F.B.I. officials in one of the larger conference rooms in the precinct. A special task force was being formed to capture the Shallow Front serial killer.

"The suspect's name is Harold Miller," Trent began. "We can probably assume, however, that that is not his real name. But we do have a physical description." Holloway tossed copies of the sketches on the table.

"So," Carl Morris, head of the U.S. Marshall team, said, "Let's nab the son-of-a-bitch."

"I'm afraid it won't be that easy," Holloway replied.

"Why not?" Agent Ramirez of the Spring Garden Drug Task Force asked.

Holloway couldn't bring himself to mention that there was a strong possibility that they were looking for God's number one adversary.

Instead, he said, "There's no file on Harold Miller. And

we have conflicting fingerprints at each crime scene."

"You're kidding," Morris said. "That's gotta be some kind of mistake."

"I wish it was," Holloway said. "But nope, no mistake and definitely not kidding. Somehow, Deputy Morris, our man can use dead peoples' fingerprints, anyone's he chooses."

Every cop in the room started speaking at once. "Gentlemen!" Holloway shouted to regain their attention. "It's fact. We can't figure out how he is doing it, but he is." Holloway grabbed a copy of each sketch and held them up. "It is also a fact that he can make himself appear as different people."

A confused silence filled the room. Holloway scanned the faces of the professional law enforcement officers and saw something he never thought he'd see. Shock, confusion and fear.

"Detective," Holloway heard. He turned and saw the drawn face of Captain Pullman.

"The meeting is over," Pullman ordered. "You need to take Officer Squall and a few other blues with you over to Lincoln."

"Why?" Holloway asked.

"Because we got a call about an hour ago. A Jack Horner called to tell us that his neighbor's door was wide open and that he found her dog killed," Pullman explained. Then he pulled Trent aside and said as quietly as he could, "The dog's owner was pregnant. And the killer left a message on the wall."

"What did it say?"

"'It ends' written in blood," Captain Pullman told him.

"OK. I'm on my way," Holloway said. He left the conference room and ran down the hall, almost knocking over the water cooler.

In ten minutes, Trent Holloway was on his way to Lincoln. Officer David Squall and his partner, Floyd Hymlan, led the way in their patrol car with sirens blaring.

Not quite a half hour after Trent left for Lincoln, Susan Edvin, the precinct clerk, received a call from a frantic woman, Sister.

"Spring Garden Police. How may I direct your call?" Susan asked politely.

"Pl-pl...please, he...help," the woman choked out.

"Ma'am, what's wrong? Do you need an ambulance?"

"N-no, I-I ne-ed to spe-speak with some-one," the woman said.

"O.K. ma'am. Just calm down and catch your breath. Tell me slowly what you need," Susan said.

"I-I-" the woman stammered.

"Go ahead, I'm still here," Susan assured the woman.

"I know where he lives!" the woman shouted.

Without asking another question, Susan instinctively knew what the woman was talking about. She waved her hands to get Lieutenant Peter Jones' attention. He was talking with a State Trooper.

The Trooper noticed Susan first and nudged Peter Jones' elbow to turn him around.

"OK, ma'am. What's your location?" Susan asked and took notes as Sister explained.

Chapter 13

Captain Pullman rounded up his team of Agent Simon Fielding and seven SWAT members. He believed that the lead was good and was sending in his finest officers to take the killer down.

The team loaded into the van and after clapping Fielding and the rest of the men on the back, Pullman watched as they pulled out into the snow.

He sighed deeply as he turned to go back to his office. He hoped the big man upstairs was paying attention today.

Holloway prepared himself for the task at hand by taking a moment to smoke a cigarette beside his unmarked police vehicle.

Squall and Hymlan waited beside him and watched as the front door to Mary Showalter's home swung back and forth with the wind.

"We going in or what?" Officer Hymlyn asked.

Holloway took a last drag and crushed the butt under his foot. "Yeah," he said with resignation.

He stepped onto the front porch and turned to the two

officers. "I want you two to question the neighbor who called in the incident," he instructed.

"Yes, sir," Officer Squall replied.

Holloway turned and entered Mary Showalter's home.

The SWAT team arrived at the condemned and abandoned apartment buildings and parked their van hidden from view. Without wasting any time, officers dressed in battle gear of bulletproof vests and Kevlar helmets jumped from the van and quickly approached the buildings in covered formation. Two officers carried riot shotguns. The other six were armed with MP-5s.

The apartment building they entered was brick. Its windows were boarded up and the front steps were crumbling. A small poster tacked to the door read DO NOT TRESPASS — BY ORDER OF SPRING GARDEN MUNICIPAL AUTHORITY.

Under it was a smaller rectangle of white paper with three words written on it.

C O M E   O N   I N

Upon closer inspection, Agent Ramirez saw that the note was skewered to the old wooden door with a carving knife, and the words were written in a crimson liquid that looked like blood.

"He knows we're here," Ramirez said as he turned to Agent Fielding. Simon gulped. *How?*

"Alright," he said. "Break the fucking door down. Be ready for anything."

"KNOCK, KNOCK!" yelled the two officers handling the battering ram as they slammed into the door. It flew open on the first attempt.

Detective Holloway stood one step inside Mary Showalter's house. He was frozen in time as he stared at the message on the door at the end of the hallway.

IT ENDS

Trent directed his flashlight at the words and saw that they were written in blood. Below them in a bloody heap on the floor was the dog. Trent panned his flashlight across the Doberman's body and saw its entrails spilling from a ghastly tear in its side. When the light reached its face, Trent was horrified to see bits of its fur clinging to its jowls.

The Antichrist did this, he thought.

With his flashlight, Trent examined the rest of the small house. Tables and chairs were upended, the television looked as if it had been thrown into the corner and every lamp had been crushed. The sofa had been ripped open and was spilling its foam guts. All the window glass had been shattered and small piles of snow had begun to collect on the cold wood floor.

Oh, Mrs. Showalter, Holloway thought, *I pity you if you're still alive.*

But Trent knew that she wasn't.

Agent Ramirez led half of the SWAT team up the stairs. Agent Fielding remained on the ground floor with the other half. Hugging the walls, they slowly made their way down the hall with guns drawn. Fielding's men had to use their flashlights to illuminate the way. It had been years since electricity lit the dark hallway. With every step, fear mingled with anticipation and each man's heart pounded in his chest.

Officer Randall Hall took a step forward and immediately raised his fist to halt the advance of the other men. Several figures loomed in the shadows not far ahead.

Fielding silently stepped forward and directed his flashlight at one.

The figure was actually a woman in a painting. She suffered from an insanity that was clearly visible in her eyes. Closer up, Fielding realized that the portrait was of Amanda Dawson, the second victim of the serial killer.

In the painting, she held hands with a tall man wearing a hat. Fielding could not see the man's eyes, but he was slicing her open while she stood naked with her mouth frozen open in a scream.

"Jesus," Agent Fielding exclaimed as he wiped sweat off his face.

"Look at this one, sir," Ramirez said in a whisper.

The second painting was a portrait of Cassandra Evans. Her terrified eyes were screaming for help. Fielding saw the reflection of the man in her dilated pupils.

"Look," Randall Hall said. He pointed his flashlight on a door with a large, rusty number hanging in the center of it, the number 6, just like in everyone's dreams.

"This is it," Agent Fielding said. The team moved into attack formation.

Who will paint for me?

"Break it down, now!" Fielding ordered. With a swift

kick, Officer Hall knocked the door completely off its hinges. It fell to the floor in a cloud of black dust.

"Move in NOW!" Fielding shouted The cops ran into the apartment, their flashlight beams cutting through the dust.

"Oh my God," Fielding said.

The room was twenty feet wide by forty feet long. Every inch of wall space was covered with dozens of paintings of tortured and mutilated women. Each painting was so red, it seemed as if it was the only color used. And in every painting, the officers found the image of the man from their dreams.

In the center of the room, a naked figure sat with his back to the SWAT team. An easel was propped in front of him. On it was another bloody work in progress.

"Hands up now, cocksucker! NOW!" Simon Fielding ordered. Instead of obeying the command, the man extended the arm holding the paintbrush and dipped it in Mary Showalter's torn open throat.

"I SAID NOW!" Fielding repeated.

The man again did not respond. Instead, he continued to paint with blood.

Ramirez was shaking as he looked at the naked, dead woman. Mary was slumped in the chair with her head thrown back to make it easier for the Antichrist to dip his brush in her bloody neck.

It looks like she's praying, Ramirez thought. *He killed her while she begged for mercy.*

"I said put your hands..." Fielding started. But before he could finish yelling the order, the naked man moved quickly to the side. Fielding and his men were too shocked by what was happening in the room that they were not prepared for what happened next.

The Antichrist grabbed Mary Showalter, his sixth victim, and hurled her across the room as if she was a trash bag.

"Jesus, look out!" Ramirez shouted.

The body sailed through the air and hit Ramirez and Fielding with a sickening wet thud. The two men were knocked to the ground. The other officers opened fire as the man fled the room but all missed hitting him. As they reloaded their guns, the Antichrist stopped, turned and blew them a kiss before disappearing.

In the next second, the building exploded. A giant plume of fire and dust reached for the sky as if it had been released after a long sentence in Hell. The explosion rattled buildings for two city blocks and thousands of windows shattered with the reverberation.

All officers but Agent Ramirez were killed instantly. He slowly burned to death.

As the rubble flew, Captain Pullman pulled up with several police cars in tow. All hopes of apprehending the perpetrator were destroyed.

"Dear Christ," was all he could manage to say.

Detective Holloway's cell phone rang.

"Holloway, here," he answered.

"Tr-Trent, this is Pullman."

By the sound of the captain's voice, Holloway knew that something terrible had happened.

"Jesus, Trent. They're, they..."

"Captain what is it? Tell me," Holloway demanded.

"They're dead, Trent. They're all dead."

"Who?"

"Come back, Trent. Come back to the station right away," Pullman finished and hung up.

Detective Holloway instructed the two officers with him to stay behind and sift through the rubble of Mary Showalter's apartment. He then jumped in his car and left behind two very frightened cops.

Firetrucks and ambulance crews worked well into the night putting out the fire and looking for clues to its origin. The investigators would never determine what caused the blast.

Harold Miller watched from a side alley. The fire had subsided to a simmering heap of red embers. Swirling hot ashes blew into the night.

At eleven o'clock that night, Trent returned home.

"Hi," he said in a grim voice. Sheila turned to see a man devastated by the horrific events.

"Was it a bomb?" she asked.

"We don't know," Trent said as he returned his wife's hug. "They pulled out the bodies, but our guy wasn't there. We think he escaped."

Sheila pulled away and looked at her husband. "Honey, let's get out of here, away from this place. I'm so afraid."

Trent fell into his easy chair and said, "Sheila, you

know I can't do that."

Sheila knew better than to push the subject. "Well, let's at least think about it. You need to do something else. You've been chasing this madman for so long. I'm afraid that he'll get the better of you," she said with sadness and concern. "What are you going to do?"

Trent fidgeted in his chair and looked at the floor. He didn't have an answer.

Chapter 14

Trent slept fitfully. The deaths of the seven policemen weighed heavily on him, and in turn, his dreams were more vivid than usual.

He stared at his reflection in the mirror. Past the five o'clock shadow and the tired eyes, he saw a man of thirty-eight, somber and sad, with lines of stress etched in his skin.

Movement behind him caught his eye, and he turned. Through a crack in the door, Trent saw a man across the room, a room he had never seen before.

The man was placing a record on an antique player. Seconds later, opera music filled the air. As he turned, Trent saw the man's face. It was Harold Miller.

Trent opened the door wider. Harold had taken hold of his dance partner's hand and had begun to dance with her. Trent expected to see Heather Mills in his dream. But instead, the woman was his wife, Sheila.

Her face was swollen and leathery, unevenly puffy and blotchy. Tears of blood streamed from the corners of her eyes.

"Noooooo!!!!" Trent screamed in his dream. He tried to run to Sheila but heard a low growl as he moved. A monster of a gray wolf pinned him where he stood.

With its head lowered, it bared its fangs at Trent. Drool dripped from its jowls onto the carpeting in foamy puddles. Trent had no doubt that the beast would rip him to shreds if he tried to run. Then he saw the chain bolted into the wall and saw that there was no slack left.

I can let go of the leash.

Trent heeded the warning he heard in his mind and didn't move a muscle as he watched the Antichrist dance with his dangling wife. Out of frustrated terror, he clamped his hands over his ears to drown out the music and closed his eyes to the horror in front of him. Fueled by his anguish, he let out a guttural scream that made the wolf whimper like a puppy.

Trent opened his eyes when he heard the telephone ring. In slow motion, he picked up the receiver

"Hello?" he said.

Silence.

"Who's there?" he asked.

"Trent. Ah Trent, don't you remember me?" a voice finally said.

"Who is this?" Trent asked again.

"I am the man you seek, Trent. I am the one who holds the leash."

Trent's mind flooded with horror. "What do you want?"

"Jeremy and Frank are here, Trent. Would you like to speak to them? Don't worry about a thing, Trent. They couldn't catch the pass either."

Trent slammed the phone down.

A brief moment later, Trent heard a bustle of activity. The door to his dark room swung open and five hospital workers entered. Two were nurses with stethoscopes. They were smiling.

"Are you feeling any better, Detective?" one asked.

"Wha-what the hell is going on?" Trent demanded to know.

"You tried to kill yourself," the doctor said with a smile. Trent saw that the doctor's teeth were jagged thorns.

Trent screamed himself awake.

Even though it was many hours from dawn, Sheila's side of the bed was empty. She had already gone to work. Trent's dream was one of the worst ones yet because she was in it. He grabbed the phone and tried to breathe as he dialed her work number. Sweat poured off of his body. He needed to be reassured that she was alright.

"Hello?" she answered on the third ring.

"Sheila?"

"Hi baby. Is everything alright?" she asked.

"Uh...yes. Everything's fine now. I just woke up from a really terrible dream."

"Are you okay?" Sheila was beginning to get worried.

"I"m, uh..." Trent stopped.

He had gotten out of bed and was looking out the window. What he saw chilled him to the bone. Outside their bedroom window, he saw footprints in the snow.

"Honey, I'll call you later. I gotta go," Trent said and hung up the phone. He quickly changed into a pair of jeans and a sweater. Moments later he was outside investigating the footprints.

He followed the trail from the woods to the house. Under the window sill, Trent could see dark earth under the packed ice. The footprints had made deep impressions as if the watcher had stood at the window a long time. But that didn't concern Trent as much as what he was looking at. One print was made by a naked human foot and the other was a hoof.

He needed to talk to Pastor Kline very badly. Kline hadn't mentioned an animal with hooves in his story.

Trent decided to walk over to the church, Even though it was cold, he needed time to think. With a cigarette between his lips and his hands buried deep in his pockets, Trent walked the streets of Spring Garden. Christmas lights twinkled in some of the windows as he made his way to the church. He smiled sadly but thankful that at least some of the citizens of his community still had some holiday spirit left in them.

Pastor Kline wasn't at the church and he wasn't at home either. Trent had been walking and thinking for over an hour and during that time, came to some conclusions.

Although every instinct told him otherwise, he couldn't deny the truth. The Antichrist did exist and was stalking the pregnant women of Spring Garden. Trent could not understand why the devil had selected his town. And he also wasn't sure why he and Sister were the only people able to see the true face of the demon. But maybe Pastor Kline could help with the answers.

Those who believe can see. But do I believe? And in whom?

It was clear to Trent that only a few people were able to see Harold Miller's true face.

"Yes," Trent said aloud as he walked down Chandler Avenue. The streetlights danced off the snowflakes and made the air around him glow.

I am the sheep among the wolves.

Across the street from Carson Park, Trent stopped to look at the wooden cross in the playground and closed his eyes against his inner turmoil.

To believe in the Antichrist, Trent knew that in the dark recesses of his heart, he must also believe in God. But Trent had been exposed to evil for so much of his life that he found it difficult to accept God. He prayed but out of habit, not true faith. God could not exist in his world because if He did, no one would be raped or murdered. If God truly existed, Trent would not be a cop, Sheila could have children, and no one would be murdering pregnant women.

But he reluctantly opened the door to believing in God. He had to. Pastor Kline had once posed a question that haunted him. If you believe in evil, must you not also believe in good? Trent did believe in evil.

Trent felt a cold breeze brush across his closed eyelids. A sudden warmer breeze followed. In a small way, he felt rewarded for opening his heart and mind to God.

"Is that a sign from you?" Trent asked as he looked up at the cross.

Suddenly, Trent heard a sound of metal scraping on the ground. In the darkness and heavily falling snow, he couldn't see its source. Whatever it was came from down the street. Trent could just barely make out a shape in the distance.

"What the hell...?" Trent asked aloud. But he already knew the answer. He closed his eyes again and prayed.

Don't let evil win, he thought.

The Antichrist approached very slowly for a final confrontation with his adversary, the cop who hunted him, the cop who would not bend to his evil will.

Holloway does not belong to me, but he will die just the same. He will die calling his wife's name... and my father's.

Harold Miller, the Antichrist, laughed.

The streetlights did not illuminate but a small circle around their bases. Their glow was a sickly yellow upon the snow. Harold Miller stepped from the darkness into one of the tight circles of light. He paused to look at Trent, eyes glowing red with blood lust and hatred. He tipped his hat and smiled.

In the next instant, Harold Miller disappeared into the night, and Holloway lost sight of him. He scanned the street but there was not another soul around.

One streetlight closer to Trent, Harold reappeared. Trent remained where he stood as the Antichrist taunted him. Then he vanished again.

Suddenly, the scraping sound Trent heard earlier was upon him. Harold Miller stood at the outer edge of Trent's own circle of streetlamp light. He rested an axe against his right leg as he struck a match to light a cigarette. The smell of burning matches brought Trent's thoughts full circle.

It's him. The killer.

"Cat got your tongue?" Harold Miller asked as he exhaled greenish smoke in Trent's direction. The smell of his breath was as repulsive as a decomposing cadaver.

"Such a shame, Detective. This is what you wanted, wasn't it?"

Trent was frozen in place, unable to answer. In his mind, he pictured the Bible and selected a prayer from his past. He recited it over and over again in his mind. *Pray for me Father and the Son and the Holy Gh...*

"Get that shit out of your head," the Antichrist whispered with a smile. He glanced at the nearest house with tiny twinkling red and white lights. They all burst into tiny fragments upon the snow. Their reflections were still visible in Harold's pupils.

Holloway looked down at the shining axe blade.

"Oh, don't mind this," Harold said as he spun it like a baton. "It's designed to separate body from mind."

Dear Jesus, I...

"You're still praying, Detective Holloway. And to what? To whom? Nothing! No one! What's it going to take to prove to you that *I* am the one true king? You've known it all along, Detective. God does not exist."

Finally Trent managed to speak, "Why," he started, "Why did you murder those women? How can you be real?"

"I am real because I am," Harold said, his eyes flickering with conceit. "And as far as those little itty bitty girls go, well, Trent my boy, I wanted to."

Suddenly, Holloway felt feverish and sick. "You killed them because you're a sick, twisted fuck."

The Antichrist jerked his head back and laughed. Blood spewed from his throat and ran down his pale skin.

"You mortals are all the same. Always wanting an explanation, a reason for everything. So tedious. But I'll tell you. It has been a long time since I discussed this particular aspect of my life with anyone. So I think I'll let you in on my little secret. I didn't care about the women at all." Trent took a step backwards as Harold Miller leaned conspiratorially closer. "All I wanted was to find the one I've been looking for, the one your God won't let me remember. My unborn son."

"Your...your son?"

"Yes. My son. In this town I smell of one who is marked, seeded. Trust me, Trent, you would not understand. I can hear my child speaking to me. He speaks to me like you speak to each other in your pathetic daily lives. He speaks to me from his mother's womb." The Antichrist saw the doubt in Trent's eyes. "He is The One, the one who will change everything you believe." Harold Miller's appearance began to change as he passionately spoke of his child.

"I need to know all of their names for the one I seek is the one name I cannot say. He is to be born again in this century. No one will know his name, not even your God."

"Bullshit!" Trent said, pulling his nine millimeter pistol from his shoulder holster. "God knows everything, demon. God knows what's gonna happen here tonight."

Harold Miller smiled and rolled his eyes back in his head. Red veined whites directed themselves at Trent.

"I will have everyone bow before me. Your mortal kind will never understand the Bible and what it truly means."

Trent cocked the hammer on his pistol and aimed it into the Antichrist's face.

"I know what the Bible means, demon. It's a death sentence for you!"

Trent fired at point blank range, three feet from the monstrous face of Harold Miller.

The man fell backwards as the back of his head exploded. Dark ruby blood splattered onto the pristine snow.

Trent stepped over the body to look at his handiwork. He screamed when he saw who Harold had become.

"No! NOOOOOOO!"

With reptilian slowness, the body the Antichrist now inhabited crawled to its knees and inched its way upright. A face Trent knew glared up at him. It was one of the faces of true evil, the face of his own father.

The body beneath the face was as tall as a man's but it was not human. Grey flesh pushed and pulled at the expensive suit jacket and shirt it wore until the fabric fell to shreds in the snow like molted skin.

As the creature transformed, Trent watched his father's face disappear in the inhumanity. It's expression was one of anger and pain but mixed with delight as if he enjoyed his time as the Devil. Trent remained where he stood, frozen in terror both past and present. He was unable to mentally grasp what he saw in front of him. Without being aware of it, he urinated in his pants.

The creature continued its mutation and flexed its new arms as if they had been bound tightly and now needed to stretch and breathe. Yet no blood flowed through its veins. They were clogged and black under the thin surface of its flaky skin. Long fingers tipped with ragged black talons extended and flexed as the creature straightened its back. Each bony vertebrae snapped and crackled as the creature grew taller and straighter. The gaping hole in the back of its head healed over with gray scales and sprouted hair as coarse as cactus spines.

Under the yellow glow of the streetlight, the metamorphosis was even more ghoulish. The rivers of red blood at the corners of the Antichrist's mouth appeared green and the whites of its eyes became repulsive neon beacons.

Detective Trent Holloway knew his death was upon him.

It ends.

Trent's body quivered as he held his pistol out in front of him again. The demon spit blood as it laughed at the puny threat.

"You're thinking about your death, aren't you Trent? You're wondering who will take care of Sheila when you're gone." The Antichrist leaned closer. Trent could feel the heat of its breath on his face.

"I will, Trent. I will take care of your darling Sheila. I haven't painted a picture of us yet."

Trent prepared himself to die. His pistol would not penetrate the creature's heart and kill it because it had no heart. Rage boiled inside of him and a fear so compelling gripped him by the balls, but he knew he was lost, that Sheila would die, too, and that the Antichrist would kill with abandon for all eternity.

The thing took a step closer. In a gravelly yet melodic voice, it said, "Your wife is so precious when she's naked. I have watched you copulate many nights, Detective, from outside your bedroom window. Her voice is so wonderful. I can't wait for her to scream for me when I skin her alive. And I will make her watch me do it. It will be such a delicious time for both of us."

The nine millimeter shook in his hand, but Holloway aimed anyway. But before he could fire, the creature's chest split open and gave birth to a two-headed wolf. Blood flew as both mouths snapped at Trent. He dropped his gun onto the gory snow.

Both wolves had the same evil eyes as the Antichrist.

Without warning, a man stepped from the shadows behind Trent. An ornate silver cross was pointed at the demon.

"Back! Back, thee devil!" Pastor William Kline shouted to the Antichrist. "BACK, HELL SPAWN! BACK, FOR YE SHALL DWELL IN YOUR OWN HOT ETERNITY! HADES HOLDS YOUR ONLY DOOR, FOR GOD'S DOOR IS CLOSED. SEPARATED FROM WINE, BLOOD AND THE RIB OF ADAM, YE WILL STAND BEFORE THE NIGHT OF WINTER IN FRONT OF LORD OUR GOD AND HE WILL ASK.

DEMON, TELL ME YOUR NAME."

The Antichrist wasted no time delivering his own message to God. He lifted Pastor Kline up by his lapels and pulled him close to his hideous face. "Look into my eyes. This is my answer to your God!"

"No! No!! Dear...God...NOOOOO!!"

William Kline looked into the eyes of the devil with all the faith he could muster and glimpsed what the Devil had in store for Earth. Great fires stretched across continents, angels impaled on hooks, corpses replacing water of the oceans, trees bleeding with disease, poverty, famine, rape and hundreds of other diabolical abuses of humanity.

"Don't worry, God's child," the Antichrist sneered. "I will save you from all this."

The twin wolves strained forward from the Antichrist's chest and attacked Pastor Kline. One ripped into his face and the other tore out his abdomen. The bloodcurdling screams of agony overwhelmed the beasts' growling. In minutes, Pastor Kline was dead. His blood streamed from his wounds onto his useless silver cross in the snow.

The Antichrist placed his mouth against William's cheek and tore it open. Then he dropped the bloody mess onto the ground between him and Trent.

Trent was barely conscious. The insanity of the scenes he had just witnessed had pushed him beyond his limit of self control. He stood before the Antichrist with the muzzle of the gun in his mouth.

"Ah, Trent. So glad you've seen the light. Join your friends. They have been waiting for you," the Antichrist said with smug satisfaction.

Trent realized that he was talking about Jeremy and Frank. *Frank. He left his wife alone. Suicide is a sin. Suicide is a sin.*

Trent snapped out of his trance and saw the cross on the ground. Maybe he had one more chance. Maybe he could destroy evil before it would destroy him.

The crucifix. It will work for me.

Reading his thoughts, the Antichrist said disappointedly, "You have one chance, Mr. Holloway. One opportunity. That is much more than I ever give. Denounce the Almighty, and I will never harm you. I will always keep hold of the leash."

Holloway picked up the cross.

"If you defy me, I will make your soul scream for death. You will watch your wife get fucked time and time again by creatures that will drive you insane when you see them. You will spend an eternity in unimaginable agony!" the Antichrist bellowed, its hideous fists pounding its chest.

Trent found his strength in the Antichrist's thinly disguised fear and empty threats.

"Fuck you, you monster!"

Trent took a step forward as the Antichrist opened its maw and leaned in for the kill. Holloway slammed the cross into the demon's mouth and shoved it down its throat. He held it there with all his might.

The demon gurgled a scream and tried to back away from the cop he couldn't control. It stumbled backwards toward the small hill behind the Lutheran church. Trent held on with all his strength. When he chanced a glance up, he saw the stained glass image of the baby Jesus not far down the hill.

"AMEN! AMEN!!!" Trent screamed as the demon tried to twist away from him.

The cross began to glow and burn in Trent's hand but he held on. The Antichrist pulled them further up the hill and was about to break free when he stumbled over the stump that William and Trent had tried to pry out of the ground.

In strange slow motion, Trent watched as the demon fell backwards on the crest of the hill and roll down the steep slope with the glowing cross in its mouth. The demon's face was pure hatred as it careened down the hill with increasing speed. At the bottom of the slope, it continued its forward momentum and flew through the air, crashing through the serene face of the baby Jesus.

Trent picked up the Antichrist's axe and ran down the hill. From where he stopped just outside the shattered window, Trent watched as the demon writhed in a mess of gore on holy ground. The thing screamed in agony as its legs melted into a puddle of dark blood.

A second later, its torso split in two. Twisted, steaming innards spilled across the hallowed church floor and sizzled in the pool of blood. The twin wolf heads reappeared, howling and thrashing, trying to free themselves from the carnage. As they dissolved in the mess, a human voice called to Trent.

"Treeeeent!" it said. The head of the demon, the Antichrist, the Devil turned to face its destroyer.

Trent screamed. Harold Holloway, his father, was now the thing on the floor.

"GET ME OUTTA HERE, SON!!!"

Trent backed away. The thing pleaded over and over again for help, for salvation. Trent cringed every time it said his name. Finally, its hair caught fire and jets of blue flame torched out of its eyes.

Harold Holloway spontaneously combusted screaming his name one last time.

"TREEEEEEEENT!!!!!!!"

Flames and smoke rose up in a thick column as the Antichrist burned. The shattered window drew the smoke out into the cold night. The flames grew hotter and stronger and exploded. Trent was knocked onto his back as a rush of smoke attacked him. A gray wolf materialized from the soot and made one final attempt to destroy Trent.

Trent reached for the axe and swung with all his might at the beast's head. The decapitated head rolled back into the church and the limp body lay on its side next to Trent.

Exhausted, Trent fell to the ground. But the Antichrist was not finished.

Behind him, the church had become an inferno. And a voice bellowed from its interior.

"I am everythiiiiing, you fool!! I am the wolves, the trees, the leaves. I am your memories! I am all the women you have ever loved. I am the sickness in your beloved's womb. I am the reason she cannot have a child!"

Trent doubled over in anguish.

"See you in Hell, son!"

Trent got up and ran from the Lutheran Church as fast as he could. The steeple had become engulfed in flames and was on the verge of collapse. Trent ran for his life but it was too late. A fire ball chased him down and struck him. A moment later, the steeple exploded and buried him in a pile of rubble.

The final snow of the long winter ahead fell that evening as fire and rescue crews battled the blaze.

The police found the mutilated body of William Kline not far from the entrance to the church. His hands were folded across his chest in a futile attempt at holding his rib cage in place. Detective Trent Holloway was found hours later under the fallen steeple.

The rescue teams worked all the night, but the killer's body was not found. They assumed that he had been consumed by the flames.

His eyes fluttered open.

A throbbing pain like he never felt before jackhammered his head. His first thought was that it was a migraine. He jolted to awareness and tried to sit up in bed. His eyes flew open but a blinding light attacked his optic nerves and he fell back in bed.

On his back, he gingerly opened his eyes again. The first thing he saw was a giant elm tree out the window, lush with dark green leaves.

Where am I?

In his peripheral vision, he saw more green. Trees. Lots of trees.

How the hell did I get here? Where's the snow?

Trent sat up and stretched his legs. He scratched the back of his head and yawned.

Slowly and deliberately, he swung his legs over the side of the bed and placed his feet on the floor. A stabbing pain shot up from his feet into his brain but he stood none-the-less. He had to see where he was.

Terror seized him, and he felt woozy.

Trent walked on wobbly legs to the door and opened it wide. Sunlight, warm and friendly, filtered through the the leaves and dappled the ground in front of him. He took a tentative step forward. *Why am I in the woods?* he thought.

He took another step forward and winced as a jagged holly leaf pricked the bottom of his foot. *Why am I barefoot?*

He looked down at his foot and noticed that he wasn't wearing any clothes either. *What the...?*

Trent remained still, frightened by his headache, thinking he must have gone on a drinking binge. Frightened because he was all alone in the woods and it was summer. *Where had the winter gone?*

He walked further into the woods with his hands folded in front of him in case he happened upon another living soul. He did not remember what had happened to him, but he did remember the demon burning in the church.

"ANYONE HERE??!!" Trent cried out. He paused, looked around and listened. No one replied, not even the birds. In fact, all was dead still and quiet.

What the fuck is going on?

Trent walked on with resolution. He wanted answers and was going to find them.

After a while, he didn't know how long, he came upon a road. Relief then embarrassment overwhelmed him. If a cop came by, how would he explain his nakedness? How would he be able to explain what he didn't understand?

But a cop didn't come along. No one did. And no one ever would.

Trent followed the road until the sun was high above the treetops. He basked in its warmth but realized that soon he would be painfully sunburned.

Where are all the cars?

"Like anyone would stop to pick up a naked man anyway," he said to himself, laughing in spite of his situation.

Trent came to a bend in the road. In the distance, he saw vibrant yellow road signs, his first encounter with humanity all day.

He quickened his pace and caught up to the signs. As he read the first sign, he slowly came to a halt.

DEAD END

He approached the other sign. An arrow pointed to the right.

He then looked away. A terrible itch annoyed him and he started to scratch it. Then he stopped.

His eyes widened. He rubbed his hands across his stomach and felt something foreign underneath his fingertips. Metal?

What the hell?

Trent slid his hand from collarbone to crotch. At regularly spaced intervals, he felt hard bumps.

What the hell? What's happened to me?

Then he understood. He began to shudder. Terror clung to him like sweat as he looked down at his body.

Staples, dozens of hard staples, evenly spaced and gleaming steel, perforated his skin. Under the staples, perfectly down the center of his body, was a long raw incision.

Trent looked at the road sign again. It now said...

ABOVE

A new sign to his left said...

BELOW

He rubbed his hand over his autopsy sutures again

and had one final thought before he screamed.

I'm dead.

Trent woke from his nightmare. His heart pounded in his chest as he threw off the thin hospital sheets.

Afraid of what he would see, he gripped the handrail and looked down. No sutures. Just oozing bandages over what he imagined were burns.

Dead men don't ooze, he thought, *or require bandages for that matter.*

He looked out the window. The site of falling snow renewed his spirit and restored him.

But would he ever really be the same? Trent thought about all that had happened to him and came to the only conclusion he could.

I've beaten the odds. It just wasn't my time to die.

And God's reward was to let him live.

"I finally caught that pass, Dad," he mumbled before drifting off once again to sleep.

Trent's recovery was truly miraculous. The doctors had not held out much hope, but there he was walking, talking, breathing. Former Detective Trent Holloway granted a few interviews with the local newspapers but declined any further involvement in the cases.

Harold Miller, who never existed, was pronounced dead at the scene of the fire even though no body had ever been found. He was blamed for all the murders in Shallow Front. The McCarthy Construction Company was hired to uproot the stump that Pastor Kline and Trent had tried to remove. Oddly, the root came out very easily in spite of the frozen conditions.

Holloway watched as they hauled it out and away. *I guess God put it there for a reason*, he thought.

The reason no longer existed.

Chapter 15

Two days after Pastor William Kline lost his battle with the Devil, Trent retired from the police force. He had had enough. A month later, he packed up his family, left his home with a For Sale sign in the front yard and started collecting his pension.

He and Sheila found a house on the ocean in Delaware. The wind swept harshly across the beach from the Atlantic but the sun was warm and soothing. Trent's most urgent plans were to do a little fishing and a lot of relaxing. Maybe he would take Detton to watch the wild ponies play in the marshes.

Try as he did, however, to forget all that he had witnessed and all that he had experienced, too many nights Trent woke up in a cold sweat with visions of Harold Miller in his mind. He tried to assure himself that the evil in Shallow Front had been destroyed. But one question continued to nag at him. Could an evil so powerful really be conquered?

Not long after the Holloways left town for good, Trent read a brief article in the local paper. Gussby Lovern had sold his tavern and, within days, was found dead in the woods. Harry Loughton was the last person to see Gussby alive. According to Harry, Gussby had gone up into the woods behind Lincoln to do some hunting. But instead of a gun, Harry said that Gussby took only a chainsaw with him. When the former tavern owner was found, he was frozen solid in the snow. Both of his arms had been cut off below the elbows and the chainsaw, found with his frozen blood crusted on the blade, was found twenty feet away.

Trent did not share the story with Sheila. He simply crumpled the newspaper, threw it in the fireplace and watched it burn.

On a sultry spring day, Trent took his wife for a drive along the coast. Detton was at school. Alone at last, Sheila asked her husband what had been on her mind since his stay at the hospital.

"Trent, do you ever think, that...um... that man will come again?" she asked nervously, her heart racing.

"No," Holloway answered.

"Are you sure, honey?"

"Yes, I'm quite sure," he said with as convincing a smile as he could manage. Inside Trent did not feel confident.

"I didn't mean to bring it up," Sheila said.

"It's fine, really. As a matter of fact, I think it's good for us to talk about it. We're far enough away from every-thing now."

"I know," Sheila replied. "Do you miss being a cop?"

Trent laughed. "Hell, no!" Then he became serious.

"Sometimes I miss Jeremy and Frank. Sometimes I miss those guys a lot, Sheila. They were my friends, good ones, the kind you don't make everyday, you know?"

Sheila reached into her husband's shirt pocket and pulled out two cigarettes. She pushed the button on the dashboard for the lighter and waited.

"What's wrong, honey?" Holloway asked. Sheila rarely smoked.

"I've been having bad dreams ever since we left Shallow Front."

"Why didn't you tell me? What kind of dreams?"

The lighter popped out, and Sheila lit her husband's cigarette and then her own. She inhaled in deeply.

"Bad ones," she said, "Awful dreams. The most God awful dreams I've ever had. I feel things, Trent. I have this feeling inside of me, like something's happened, that I just can't explain."

"Try?" Holloway coaxed. "I want to know."

"Don't you mean you need to know?" Sheila asked. "Let's face it, Trent, this has been all about you, hasn't it?"

Holloway said nothing as they drove along the gray strip of road.

"Jeremy's in them."

That surprised Trent.

"And Frank's in them, too."

Trent quickly glanced at his wife and saw her eyes were glistening.

Sheila continued, "Goddammit, Trent. As soon as I close my eyes at night, there they are!"

Sheila pushed her hair off her forehead, took a drag of

her cigarette and regained her composure.

"Every dream is the same. Jeremy Harris is walking down the road. I know he's dead, but he's walking toward our house just the same. And not our old house on Calldown Boulevard but the one right here in Delaware. I'm asleep but I wake up and go to the screen door. I hear him coming, walking on the crushed sea shells in our driveway."

"I'm listening," Holloway said.

"I go outside onto our front porch and he's there with Frank. And his eyes are gone. I don't know what happened to them. And on his shirt are the words CAR CRASH. They look like they were written in blood. I see glass from the windshield twinkle in his hair and some big, jagged pieces are sticking out of his face and skull. And his eyes are gone."

Holloway almost jerked the wheel.

"Beside him is Frank and he's smiling. God, Trent, he's smiling and it's awful. I can see fire in his eyes. Then he turns his wrists upward and slowly raises his arms to show me the cuts he made."

"Oh my God, Sheila."

"And then next to them, next to your friends, is this big dog that stops when they stop. But when I get a better look, I see that it's not a dog at all."

Holloway suddenly felt nauseous.

"It's a wolf, the most evil looking wolf you ever laid your eyes on. And when it sees me, it splits its muzzle open to show me its long, jagged teeth," Sheila shuddered. "I close the door quickly and stay inside but I still watch. The wolf tilts its head at the sound I make just like a dog would. But what chills me most is that Jeremy and Frank do the same thing at the exact same time the wolf does it. Then the wolf speaks."

"What does it say?" Holloway asked.

Sheila tossed her cigarette out the window and looked at her husband.

"It says...." but she couldn't continue and broke down crying.

"Sheila, please tell me."

Through her sniffles, Sheila told him. "It says 'You can't hide him from me.'"

"What do you suppose that means, Trent? Why am I dreaming these things?"

Holloway lied. "I don't know, honey."

"Is that all you have to say? You don't have anything else to offer?" Sheila was stunned.

"Honey, it has taken everything I have upstairs," he said as he pointed to his head, "to keep from going insane over the whole ordeal. I need to keep it locked away. Too many people died. I can't dwell on it anymore."

Sheila stared out the window. "Sorry. I know you don't want to talk about it. And I really don't want Detton to know, but..."

Sheila turned away from her husband. A sob heaved in her chest, and a second later, she was crying.

"Hey, what's wrong?" Holloway asked. He pulled onto the sandy shoulder of the road and reached for his wife.

"I can't have kids," she sobbed. Trent pulled a Kleenex from the box they kept on the back seat for Detton and wiped her runny nose.

"I know, honey. Why bring it up now? We have Detton

and he..."

"I know, Trent. I know. He's wonderful. It's not about him," Sheila said. "I can't have children. The ovarian cancer stole that from me. But even so, I've always hoped for a miracle. That on that day each month, I would wake up and not bleed."

Sheila cried harder as Trent held her tighter and stroked her hair.

"I'm sorry," she sniffled through her tears.

"You have to face facts, Sheila. You have..."

"Trent!" Sheila interrupted, "I have faced facts! That's what I'm trying to tell you!" She sighed and turned to look at her husband with red rimmed eyes.

Trent looked into them and knew something was terrifying his wife.

"You told me that the dark man, the Devil, was looking for his child, his unborn child. Right?" Sheila asked.

"Yes, I did. I should have never have told you..."

"He never found what he was looking for, right?" Sheila asked again.

Trent nodded.

"I'm late, Trent..."

Holloway froze. "What? What do you mean 'you're late'?" Fear swept over him like a tidal wave.

"I'm pregnant!!!"

The truth hit Trent like a ton of bricks. Somehow the Antichrist had gotten to his wife, had gotten into his wife.

It wasn't physically possible for Sheila Holloway to conceive a child, yet she did.

Trent gripped her for what felt like hours. Storm clouds rolled in from the east over the whitecapped waves and churned the water a ominous gray.

He didn't know what would happen now. He just expected it to rain.

Teri Woods Publishing
an Entertainment Investment Group

ORDER FORM

Teri Woods Publishing
Greeley Square Station
P.O. Box 20069
New York, NY 10001-0005
www.teriwoods.com

TELL ME YOUR NAME	**$14.95**
Shipping/handling (via U.S. Priority Mail)	**$ 3.85**
TOTAL	**$18.80**

Order additional titles from TWP: YES

True to the Game by Teri Woods	$14.95	☐
B-More Careful by Shannon Holmes	$14.95	☐
The Adventures of Ghetto Sam and The Glory of My Demise by Kwame Teague	$14.95	☐
Dutch by Teri Woods	$14.95	☐
Triangle of Sins by Nurit Folkes	$14.95	☐

Purchaser Information

Name _____

Reg.# _____

Address _____

City _____ State _____ Zip _____

Total number of books ordered _____

For orders shipped directly to prisons, TWP deducts 25% of the sale price of the book. Costs are as follows:

TITLE OF BOOK	$11.21
Shipping/handling	$ 3.85
TOTAL	$15.06